THE RECKONING

A SHATTERED ISLE NOVEL

JADE PRESLEY

ALSO BY JADE PRESLEY

The Shattered Isle series

Her Villains

Her Revenge

The Assassins

Her Mates

AVAILABLE IN AUDIO!

Her Villains

Her Revenge

PATREON

Want exclusive perks like first access to books, fan art, premium swag, live chats with me, and more? Check out my Patreon tiers and see which one works for you!

Find all that and more here!

CONTENT WARNING

This book contains some depictions of emotional abuse, violence, and explicit sexual content with multiple consenting partners. I've taken every effort to handle these issues sensitively, but if any of these elements could be considered triggering to you, please take note.

To all my amazing, supportive readers.
I'm with you, till the end of the line.

1

LOCK

"How many did you bring in today?" Huxton, the leader of the Onyx City, asks as he offers me a large goblet of wine. He slides the golden cup across the smooth ebony table in one of his many council rooms.

I lean up from my chair, exhaustion clinging to my bones as I reach for the offering and take a large gulp. The sparkling liquid does little to reinvigorate my powers, but they're on their last dregs.

"Two-hundred and sixty-three," I say, and Huxton's golden eyes widen.

"Stars," he says, shaking his head. "Have you slept?"

I pause with the goblet poised at my lips, my eyes on the swirling liquid inside as I shake my head. "*She* hasn't," I say, taking another generous gulp.

My mate.

My beautiful, ruthless mate.

She nor Gessi have slept since that forsaken box was sent to our chambers in Jasmine Falls.

Four nights. Four days. It's been a never-ending cycle

where our efforts were split. Steel and I flying to one village or city in need, Gessi and Cari to another, Gessi's mates to another, saving as many as we can.

"You need rest," Huxton says, leaning back in his chair.

Thank the stars for him, for his formidable city. We wouldn't have had anywhere to take those we saved if it weren't for him.

"I will," I say, setting down the now-empty glass. "When she does." I tap the glass, pushing back from the table. "Thank you for that," I say, standing before him. "For all of it." Normally I'm not one for bouts of vocalized gratitude, but he's earned it. A true ally, one even the All Plane will never forget.

"Like I told your queen and mine," he says, rising to walk with me out of the room. "We are with them."

The shadows in my blood flicker with starvation, as if they've been deprived the basic needs of water and food and oxygen. I'm drained, so very drained, but with my abilities of transporting people through the shadows, I was the only one capable of saving so many.

And I wouldn't damn these people because I needed a fucking nap.

"Are there any more?" Huxton asks as we stop outside the room he's given Cari. Steel and myself have rooms of our own too, but I want to be with my mate.

Talon and Tor will eventually make the trip to the Onyx City, once they ready the All Plane soldiers we can spare.

"No," I say. "I think that's the last of them." I rest my hand on the door handle, feeling almost too weak to turn it, to remain standing, but I don't dare let it show.

Thirteen thousand. We saved about thirteen thousand among the tens of thousands who suffered the recent attacks wrought by the general. He'd bided his time. Waited until he had the throne, to show his hand.

His army is formidable and the sky ships and weapons he's gathered are even more so...we still haven't figured out who is supplying him.

"Good," Huxton says, knowing better than to reach out to me, to do something as foolish as grip my shoulder in support. He's smarter than that, but I see it in his eyes, feel it along the edges of his mind that I'm too tired to protect against. "My people will care for them, find places for all of them," he says. "You need to rest. Your queen does too. They all do."

I nod, feeling as if he breathed too hard I would fall over.

I've never pushed myself this hard for this long.

Huxton gives me another nod, then heads down the hallway, his long gait eating up the space in no time, leaving me alone outside my door.

Finally, I turn the handle and step into the room, my vision blurring around the edges as I close the door behind me.

"Cari," I say when I see her through the fog in my eyes. She's gorgeous, but brutally exhausted. The skin beneath her eyes is now a deep indigo rather than the glittering blue I'm used to.

She looks up briefly, smiling at me before she continues doctoring a wound on her arm, a cut just beneath her night-blooming-flower tattoo, the thin black lines of ink now stained with blood.

I furrow my brow, instinct roaring, blaring to go to her, but I can't move.

I can't make my feet move.

"Cari," I say again, the world tilting on its axis.

I drop to my knees, the breath rushing from my lungs.

"Lock!"

Cari calls my name.

I hear her rushed footsteps toward me, but I can't see her anymore.

There is nothing but darkness.

My shadows curl inside me, *around* me, and jerk me backward down a long tunnel with no end in sight.

2

CARI

"**L**ock!" His name rips from my lips as I race across the room, my exhausted muscles not moving quick enough.

Lock hits the floor with an audible thud, and I slide on my knees, crashing against him as I draw his head in my lap.

"Lock!" I push his long black hair away from his face. "Lock, wake up. Wake up!"

He doesn't move beneath my touch.

Panic slices through my veins as I run my hands over his body, checking for injuries. There are no visible wounds. "Lock," I beg, shaking him.

Nothing.

"Steel!" I cry out as loud as I can, fear rooting me to the spot. I can't leave him to go get help, I *can't*.

Steel crashes through the bedroom door, muscles tense and chest heaving as he scans the room, looking for the threat. His face falls when he sees Lock in my arms, and he drops to his knees beside me.

"What happened?" he asks, checking over Lock in the

same way I did, but taking it one step further and checking his vitals with a calm efficiency I don't possess.

"I don't know," I say, my voice hoarse. "He walked in and then just collapsed."

Steel tilts his head, his blue eyes locking with mine. "His breathing is steady."

A sliver of relief snakes through the endless well of panic blasting through me. "Where was he just now?" I ask, hating that I don't know. I'd been in here, cleaning a wound from the most recent battle. Gessi and I had saved a few hundred people from the orchard district and paid for their lives with blood of our own.

"He'd brought back the last of the survivors, almost three hundred of them—"

"Three hundred?" I cut him off. "He transported that many?"

Steel nods, hefting Lock from my arms and carrying him to the bed.

He could be sleeping, he looks that at ease. But something is terribly wrong. I can feel it in my bones, in the connection that binds us as mates—it's fuzzy, almost like someone has numbed it.

"What did he do after he came back?" I ask.

"He met with Huxton—"

"I'll fucking kill him," I snap, rage pulsing through me as I stomp out the door and down the luxurious hallways of Huxton's palace in the Onyx City.

"Cari!" Steel calls, racing after me, but I ignore him, turning a corner to find—

"You!" I spot Huxton speaking to Gessi just outside his favorite dining hall. His golden eyes fly wide as I slam into him, my fingers iced over as I grip his throat. "What did you *do*?"

Huxton holds his hands up, not fighting back even as I increase the pressure against his throat.

"Cari," Steel says, his voice like a beacon of reasoning. "Let him speak," he says, sliding his fingers over the arm I have flexed until he reaches my hand and gently pulls it away.

Huxton gasps, sucking in a sharp breath.

Gessi comes to stand on my left while Steel flanks my right.

"You have one chance, Huxton," I say, angry tears welling in my eyes. My powers are thrashing, begging me to slice into him, into *someone*. To make whoever did this to Lock pay.

His eyes go distant as he reaches across time and space, sorting through information and events in a way I still can't fully comprehend. "Lock," he says, understanding shaping his features as he snaps back to the present. "He's been harmed."

"You were the last person to speak with him," Steel says, standing close enough to Huxton that he can't possibly escape, not that he's trying.

Huxton rubs at his throat as he nods. "Just a few moments ago, yes," he admits, then shakes his head. "I didn't hurt him, Cari."

"What. Happened." I can barely form words, my mind spinning with the possibility of losing Lock.

"He told me how many people he brought back," Huxton hurries to say. "Then we shared a drink and I told him to get some rest...that he'd done enough."

An ice dagger forms in my hand, and I raise the tip of the blade to his throat as I step closer. "I will kill you where you stand," I say. "I'll make it quick if you tell me what you put in that drink."

Hurt flashes through his eyes, and a small, *tiny* pang of guilt twists my heart at the look. Huxton has been nothing but kind to me, to the Shattered Isle people we've brought back to flood his city streets. He's saved them, saved us...but I'm blinded by the loop of Lock collapsing over and over in my mind.

"Sparkling wine," Huxton says carefully, barely moving so the blade doesn't nick his skin. "I have never given you a reason to believe I would betray you, Cari. *Never.*"

The angry tears building in my eyes spill over, rolling down my cheeks, but I don't drop the knife. I'm a torrent of emotions, fear and panic and grief already doing their best to consume me.

"Cari," Gessi says from behind me. "I believe him. He's welcomed all of our people into his city without complaint, without demands—"

"I know that," I snap, and immediately cringe. I never speak to Gessi with such rage. "But he's the last one to see Lock—"

"Steel," Huxton cuts in, eying my mate. "What happened on the rescue mission? Did anything unusual occur?"

How can Huxton think rationally when his life is in my hands? How can he sound so calm when all I can think about is my world crumbling around me?

"It was gritty," Steel explains. "We had to fight our way through a dozen of the general's guards each. And then the people were in a panic, understandably. They rushed us. Some were begging for help, others were blaming us for coming too late..." His voice trails off, and the pain in it makes me turn to look at him.

My mate, the heart of all our bonds. He's taking those words personally, blaming himself for the extreme losses the Isle has suffered even though it's all the general's doing. Something snaps in his eyes, his head tilting.

"Oh, Sun above," he says, a muscle in his jaw flexing. "There was a survivor." His words are hurried, his eyes somewhere else as he relives the moment. "He was the only one who managed to get his hands on Lock. He looked like he was thanking him. I swore I saw something in his hand, but it was too quick. And Lock didn't react other than shoving him off. You know how he hates praise or gratitude—"

"Where is this survivor?" I ask, my dagger falling as I take a step away from Huxton.

"Come," Huxton says. "The most recent batch of survivors are still in processing in the great hall."

We make it to the great hall in minutes, our intense entry startling the survivors who are in four separate lines to collect provisions—fresh clothes, a blanket and pillow, food and water, and an appointment card with Huxton's staff to set them up with work when they're ready.

"Show me," I demand.

Steel scans the crowd, his entire body tensing when he spots a man across the room at the back of the third line, fidgeting as he shifts from one foot to the other.

"Him," he says, stepping forward, already making his way through the crowd.

The man spots the commotion, and *bolts* at the sight of Steel.

I think fucking not.

I sprint ahead, intercepting the runner. I slam into him, the force of our impact sending us sliding across the polished floors of the great hall until we smack against the wall. I roll atop him, barely gaining my balance before I slam my fist into his face.

Again.

And again.

My knuckles burn, the skin splitting.

I barely feel it.

"Tell me what you did to him!" I scream, throwing another punch.

The man laughs. He fucking *laughs*.

"Cari!" Steel's arms wrap around me from behind, hauling me away.

The man scrambles to stand, but thick green vines wrap around his wrists and ankles, rooting him to the spot.

I flash Gessi a thankful glance, then shake off Steel.

"Killing him won't get us answers," Steel says, and I take a deep breath to try to slow the adrenaline begging me to cut into this man.

"You might as well," the man says, spitting blood on the floor. "I'll never tell you."

I fly forward and punch him again, relishing the satisfying sound of his jaw crunching beneath my fist.

Steel steps in front of me, towering over the man. "You will tell me everything."

The man has the audacity to smile up at Steel as if he just invited him to the All Plane palace. "I'll die first."

"That can be arranged," I snap.

Steel turns to Gessi. "When will Blaize be back?"

"An hour," she answers.

"I have detainment cells," Huxton offers from behind me.

Steel nods, grabbing the bound man and hauling him across the room like he's nothing more than a blanket bundle. "Show me, please," Steel says, and Huxton motions the way.

I follow until we're out of the great hall, where Steel pauses. "Go be with Lock," he says, and my eyes flare wide. He lowers his voice. "Blaize will get it out of him. I promise. Trust me."

"He's right," Gessi offers.

I sigh, the weight of what's happened sinking atop my chest. I look to Huxton, parting my lips. I almost killed him. I shake my head, unable to form the words—

"It's all right," he says, his golden eyes sincere. "I promise. I understand."

I blow out a breath, and Gessi takes my hand, leading me back to my room as Steel and Huxton and the survivor disappear the opposite direction.

"Blaize is the best," she says. "He'll get the information we need and then we can help Lock."

I don't have the energy to respond, so I just nod and lean into her as she opens my door.

A female stands on the side of my bed, a needle sunk into the crook of Lock's arm.

"What the hell are you doing?" I snap.

"What the hell does it look like I'm doing?" she asks, gently sliding the needle from his arm, collecting a vial of his blood. She quickly slides a bandage over the small wound before pocketing the vial.

She turns to face us, and I arch a brow at her. She's stunning, with smooth lavender skin, long wavy red hair that falls over the practical clothes she wears, and stunningly dark eyes.

"Who are you?"

"Wynter," she answers, rounding the bed to stand before us. "Huxton called me while you were storming the great hall." She motions her head behind her, toward Lock.

"You're a healer?" I ask, hope blossoming in my chest. "Can you help him?"

"Not a healer, exactly," she says, shrugging. She's way too calm and casual for my liking at the moment. "Huxton calls me his witch, but really I'm just his assistant with a penchant for science and a talent for...well..." She grins, curling her fingers in front of my face—

A crystal-clear image of Gessi and myself forms right in front of us, as if we've been duplicated. Gessi waves her hand through her doppelganger and it passes right through it.

"Illusionist," I whisper.

The power is rare. It's like Lock's ability to alter minds, but outwardly.

"Among other things," Wynter says, closing her hand into a fist. The illusion disappears. "Now, girl talk is fun and all, but I need to get this back to my lab." She pushes past us, and I whirl around, stopping her at the door.

"Thank you," I say, instead of doing what a queen should do—chide her for being so blunt and informal, but I simply don't have the energy to be the royal version of myself right now.

"Don't thank me yet, queen," she says. "I tried getting in his head," she admits. "It's blocked in a way I've never seen before. I have no idea what I'm up against."

I swallow hard, my chest tightening.

"But I'll tell you the second I figure it out."

I dip my head to her before she turns out of the room, shutting the door behind her. I lean against it, sliding to the floor, and unleash the sob I've been keeping at bay.

Gessi slips her arms around me, joining me on the floor.

I cling to her, using her support to ground me when I feel like my world is spiraling.

Because my mate is in that bed, so close but so incredibly far away...

And I don't know if I'll ever get him back.

3

BLAIZE

It's been a while since I've broken someone.

I've missed it.

"You're putting up a valiant effort," I say as I circle the male. "But if you're looking for praise, I'm not going to give it to you."

The male is half slumped in the chair he's tied to, his arms stretched tight behind his back, his ankles secured at the bottom. I glance over my shoulder, to where my mate watches from beyond the bars of the cell Huxton threw the traitor in an hour ago.

Gessi's eyes are locked on me, and I can feel her mixture of worry and desire pulsing down the bond that connects us. My mention of *praise* has her thinking wildly inappropriate thoughts under the current circumstances.

I didn't think it was possible, but I fall even harder for her.

"Now, let's try again." I take my focus off Gessi, flashing a quick, silent look at Steel, who leans in the corner of the dank cell, his arms folded over his chest. Worry etches the lines of his eyes, but not where anyone outside of me or Cari would notice. "What did you do to Lock?"

The male shakes his head, sweat soaking his shirt. The color of his clothes is plain and he has no identifying marks on his skin. He could just as easily be a disgruntled Shattered Isler hell bent on harming an All Plane king as he could be working for the general.

That's what I'm here to find out—that, and what the hell he gave Lock to put him down. It had to be something incredibly strong. I've known Lock as long as I have Steel, and that man could take out entire battle regiments in his sleep. Whatever took him down has to be powerful and most likely new.

That fact points more to the general than someone working alone out of spite against the All Plane kings, but I won't know until he breaks.

I bend at the waist, enough to catch the male's eyes. "You see this?" I ask, pointing to the floor and making circles in front of him. He follows where I indicate, then glares up at me. "Do you see any of your blood?"

He shakes his head, and a lethal grin slips over my lips.

"That's because I can hurt you a thousand different ways without making you bleed."

Spit splatters against my cheek.

I exhale a long, slow breath, my hands curling into fists before I wipe off the offense.

Steel pushes off the wall, but I hold up a hand to stop him.

"That's one," I say, lashing out to grip his chin between my fingers. He whimpers as I increase the pressure. With half a thought, I could rip off his entire jaw. My strength matches Steel's, but the tattoos covering my arm? The silver and red are drenched with an ancient magic I don't think I'll ever fully understand, but I sure as hell appreciate at times like this.

They're a blessing and a curse from the previous All Plane king. Steel's father forced them on me years ago to help me be a better assassin for him.

I shove the thoughts away, my blood sizzling with the power I hold over this piece of shit.

"So," I say, releasing him so harshly his head snaps to the left. "How many other ways would you like to hurt?" I cock a brow. "We're only on method number twenty-six."

He looks up at me, eyes narrowed. He's got a backbone, I'll give him that.

And I'll be happy to break it for him too, if he keeps up the pompous act.

"Why do they always choose the hard way?" I ask Steel.

"Stupidity," Steel answers as he walks to my side. "Blaize always wins," he says, eying the male. "It would be a lot easier if—"

"How does it feel?" It's the first time in an hour that the male has spoken out of turn.

I share a quick look with Steel.

"How does *what* feel?" Steel asks, playing into it.

"How does it feel to know you're going to lose your brother?"

I barely move in time to stop Steel—he's that fast.

He slams into me, ready to tear this guy's head off. I wrangle him back, shaking my head.

That's what he wants. I silently convey the words once I catch Steel's gaze.

Prisoners always look for quick ways to die, to eliminate the chance of breaking and telling us what we need to know.

Steel shakes me off, spinning around to catch a breath.

I whirl around, crossing the distance between me and the target in a matter of breaths.

I grip his wrist, applying just the right amount of pressure—

He wails, stomping his feet as he desperately tries to get away from me.

He can't.

I squeeze harder, my heart pounding against my chest as adrenaline courses through my veins.

A loud crack sounds over his wailing, seconds before the bone gives beneath my fingers.

I sigh, satisfied as I drop his hand and take a step back.

He whimpers through clenched teeth.

"Let's try again," I say, exasperated. Steel is right, they all fold in the end. It would be so much quicker if they realized that in the beginning. "Who ordered the attack against the All Plane king?"

Tears roll down the male's cheeks as he glares up at me.

"Don't look at me like that," I say, barely able to hold in a vicious laugh. "All that anger you're feeling? All that unkempt rage?" I point to him. "Direct it at yourself. I've given you every opportunity to speak to us without painful incentive. To have a conversation instead of a confrontation. You're the one in control here. All you have to do is tell me who ordered the attack and what you gave him, and I'll leave." I shrug. "I bet you'll see a healer and have a meal. Huxton is a nice, cushy ruler like that."

"Untie my arms," he says, out of breath. "It fucking hurts."

I watch him for a few more moments.

"Untie my arms," he begs. "I'll tell you, but untie them first."

I take my time considering the request, pacing the small

space before him. He has a broken wrist, three broken ribs, and a fractured shin. He's certainly not going to get the upper hand on me, not to mention Steel, if that's what he's thinking. Hell, Gessi would slice him in half with one of her deadly vines before she let him get anywhere near either of us.

"If I untie you and you choose not to tell me what I want to know, your good hand is the first thing you'll lose."

He nods, sighing deeply as I cut away his bonds with my knife. I pocket the blade in a holster on my thigh before looking down at him again.

"Who ordered—"

"The general," he cuts me off, spitting on the floor. "Of course, it was the general."

An icy stone sinks to the pit of my stomach. I knew, deep down, I think we all knew, but I didn't think the bastard could reach us so easily.

"How—"

"He's always going to be one step ahead of you, you know that, don't you?" he asks, smirking up at me with an entitled grin that makes me want to rip off a limb. "He knew what would happen the second he claimed the throne. He's had us positioned for weeks."

"Us," I say, nodding. "How many more of you are there?" Enemies hiding amongst those who needed to be saved. A clever plan. Evil, but clever.

"Infinite," he answers.

I roll my eyes, leaning down a bit to focus on him. "A hundred?"

He doesn't flinch.

"Two hundred?"

Pride fades from his features.

"Oh, that was too high," I say, and his smugness falls

instantly.

"Fifty?"

Nothing.

I laugh, shaking my head. "Twenty?"

A muscle in his jaw ticks.

"Twenty," I say over my shoulder toward Steel.

"Are they all here?"

"You'll never know until it's time to know," the male says. "You All Planers are all the same. Arrogant, entitled assholes who think they know everything."

I raise my brows, feigning shock. "That was mean," I say. "I'm definitely not entitled."

A small, surprised laugh echoes from behind me, and I spare a glance at Gessi. Her delicate, emerald fingers cover her lips, but I can see the laughter in her eyes.

I smile at her, my heart doing all sorts of weird things at knowing my mate is here, watching me without fear. I didn't know that could exist for me.

"What did you give the All Plane king?" I ask, turning my attention back to him.

He's shaking now, the entirety of his body trembling as the veins in his neck flex beneath his skin. "I gave him," he says, his breathing erratic. "This!"

His good hand flies forward, a syringe slicing through the air, aimed just over my shoulder and headed directly for—

Gessi.

Instinct has me flying backward, moving as fast as I possibly can as I reach, plucking the syringe out of the air just a centimeter before it would've punctured her skin.

"Oh, fuck," Steel breathes the words.

But I barely hear him, can barely think as I toss him the syringe, my eyes solely focused on the male.

"My mate." I yank the male's head back with one hand, drawing back my silver arm with the other. "That was aimed at my fucking *mate*." I punch through his chest in one clean, hard motion, clenching my eyes shut as the warm, sticky innards of his chest sucks on my arm.

Gessi gasps behind me, but I snap my eyes open, focusing on the male as I rip out his heart and show it to him.

His eyes are confused and hazy before they go wholly lifeless.

He slumps to the left, his entire body smacking against the floor, the steady *drip, drip, drip* of his blood leaking from my fist.

I unclench it, and his heart thwacks against the floor next to his body.

Assassin.

Killer.

Monster.

The words pulse in my mind to the beat of my racing heart. I glance down at my hands, now covered in sticky red, and I cringe against the onslaught of memories that hit me.

So much blood.

Not all of it evil.

All on my hands.

Spiders crawl along my skin, making my muscles itch as shame and guilt swirl inside me.

But not for this asshole.

Not when he just tried to kill my mate.

I swallow down the memories, the doubts, the emotions, and spin around.

Steel is there, checking on Gessi with a supportive hand on her arm, but she only has eyes for me.

I expect her to scream. To scold me. To run in terror.

Fuck, I never meant to show her this side of myself. I never wanted my mate to know the things I'm capable of—

"Blaize," she whispers, gently pushing away from Steel and walking toward me. Her steps are timid as she reaches for me. "Come here," she demands as she extends her hand for mine.

I look at the blood coating my fingers, and shake my head.

She sighs and grabs my hand anyway.

Fire slices through the icy shame coating my insides, cutting right through the fear of scaring my mate away as she touches me without hesitance.

"Steel," Gessi says as she tugs me toward the hallway. "Please get that to Huxton and Wynter as quickly as possible." She eyes the syringe in his hand, and Steel blinks out of the death stare he's been giving the lifeless male.

"Right," Steel says, coming back to himself. He gently clutches my shoulder. "Thank you," he says before rushing past us.

Gessi walks us slowly through Huxton's palace, giving anyone who looks at me sideways a death glare of her own.

It's not until we make it into our bedchamber that I let out a tight breath.

"Gessi," I say, shaking my head. I want to say I'm sorry, but I'm not. Am I sorry she witnessed me going full assassin on him? Yes, absolutely. But I'm not sorry the son of a bitch is dead. I'd do it again.

And anyone who even breathes the wrong way toward Gessi will meet the same fate.

"Come on," she says, her hand still in mine as she leads me into the bathing chamber.

She turns on the hot water in the massive black-stone shower before turning to face me. Gently, with fingers now coated in the same blood that drenches mine, she starts removing my clothes.

"Gessi," I say again, my brow furrowed as she tosses my clothes in a garbage bin in the corner. She sheds her dress, the beautiful blue splattered with red. "What are you doing?"

Her eyes flicker up to mine. "I'm taking care of you." She says it so matter of factly.

"You...you shouldn't be. I don't deserve—"

"Hush now," she cuts me off. "None of that." There is a challenge in her eyes that has me cocking a brow.

"You're honestly telling me that didn't terrify you?" I ask as she pulls me into the shower.

"Of course it did," she says, pushing against my chest until we're both under the stream of hot water.

I swallow hard, nodding. I half expect her to flinch when I reach for the soap behind her, but she doesn't. She merely takes the bar out of my hand, creating a lather between her fingers before working the suds over my hands. Carefully, she massages each one, working the lather until it turns pink as it washes the blood off our hands.

I don't think I'm breathing as I watch her.

She's stunning, and the bond between us is pulsing with nothing but love and desire and...

"Why are you sad?" I ask, as she guides my hands under the water, rinsing them clean. Then she gets to work on my body.

She works her hands over my arms, rubbing the tense muscles until they loosen. Her breasts graze my chest as she continues to move the lather over my body, but her eyes flicker up to mine. "I'm sad because I caused a problem for you," she admits.

"What?" I ask, shaking my head. "No, you didn't."

"I did," she says, smoothing the lather over my abdomen. Fuck, her hands are like magic as they work me over. "If I hadn't been there, he wouldn't have had a chance to try and hurt me, and then you wouldn't have had to do what you did."

"That's not true," I say. "I would've done it either way."

She purses her lips, contemplative as she skims her fingers over my hips. "Okay then."

I tip her chin to meet my eyes. "What do you mean *okay then?*"

She shrugs. "Okay then," she says again. "If it wasn't my presence that caused your reaction, then I'm glad I was there to support you in the aftermath."

Shock reverberates through me, and she must feel it down our bond because she gasps. Her brow furrows, and she shakes her head. "Why are you surprised?" she asks, drawing a hand up to my cheek. "I love you, Blaize." She taps my cheek, a luscious grin on her lips. "And not just for this exquisite face."

I huff a dark laugh.

"I love every piece of you. The light and the dark. The fun and the terrifying," she says, wetting her lips. "You're my mate. You no longer have to shoulder these burdens alone."

Emotions tangle in my throat as she holds my gaze.

How many times have I had to suffer alone after an ordered kill? How many times have I almost let the icy cold consume me after doing what I must?

And how in the fuck did I land a mate like her?

"Now, you're all clean," she says, dropping her hands, her eyes skimming over every inch of my body. The hot water soaks us both, steam wafting around us in waves.

"You are the perfect mate," I say, leaning down to capture her mouth with mine. She opens willingly, letting me in to sweep my tongue over hers. Sun above, kissing her is like coming home. All the jagged pieces of me right themselves, our bond flaring between us like a perfect beacon to bring me back from the darkness.

But I can live as myself and know she stands with me no matter what. That's a feeling I never knew existed.

Gessi breaks our kiss, her eyes laced with lust as she drops to her knees and wraps her lips around my cock.

"*Fuck*," I growl, my chest heaving with a shocked breath. "Gessi."

I tangle my fingers in her hair, resting my head against the warm stone wall, water spilling over my shoulders and down atop of her. The sensations mix as she sucks me deeper into her mouth, successfully emptying my head of all thought.

Nothing exists outside of her.

Outside of the way she feels. All hot and slick as she sucks and swirls her tongue along my cock, teasing and pumping me until every single muscle clenches with need.

My mate.

My mate just watched me rip out a traitor's heart, and instead of running away from me, she's on her knees for me.

Fucking hell.

She takes me all the way in, my cock bottoming out in her throat, and I hiss, looking down at her.

Her eyes are on me, molten and needy as she sucks me down over and over. The sight threatens to make my knees buckle, threatens to have me coming down her throat in a matter of seconds.

But that can't happen.

I gently tug on her hair, my cock sliding from her mouth with a satisfying little pop. She licks her lips like she can't get enough of my flavor, and lava shoots through my veins.

"My turn," I say, hauling her to her feet and higher, until she locks her ankles around my back.

Fuck, she feels amazing. The water has made our skin slick, and her heat slides over my cock like silk. I turn, pressing her spine against the wall, and she hisses from the quick bite of cold against her skin. I hold her there with one arm tucked beneath her ass while I reach between us with my free one.

"Blaize," she moans when I grip my cock and glide it through her heat. She rocks against me, eager to feel me inside her.

"Not yet," I say, tugging myself out of her reach. I slant my mouth over hers, swallowing her little whimpers of protest. "Not until you come on my fingers first."

I slide two fingers inside her, relishing her gasp of surprise. Fuck, she's drenched and squeezing me so tight. My cock begs me to sink into her, but I ignore it. This is about her.

I pump her, using the arm I hold her with to heft her up and down, giving her all the leverage she needs to ride my hand.

"Blaize," she groans, tangling her fingers in my hair to the point of pain.

Fuck, I love it when she does that. Love it when she says my name like that. Love every fucking thing about her.

I increase my pace in the way only my tattooed fingers can do, and she rips her mouth away from mine, her head arching back against the wall. She's gorgeous like this, all sensation and instinct, all flushed and achy for me.

"That's it," I say, feeling her tighten around me as her body rides that edge. "You're going to come on my fingers," I continue. "And then I'm going to fuck you so hard, you won't be able to stand the rest of the night."

Gessi whimpers, reduced to unintelligible groans as I push her right over the edge.

"Blaize!" she cries my name as she shudders around me, her desire sliding down around my fingers to join the water crashing all around us. I work her through the throes of it before gently sliding my fingers out of her and bringing them to my lips.

Fuck, she's delicious. A refreshing taste like spring water and mint and pure Gessi, her earth powers radiating through every inch of her.

"Good girl," I say, barely giving her time to catch her breath before I slam my cock inside her.

"Stars!" she gasps, wrapping her arms around my neck to draw me even closer.

She's searing silk as I pull all the way out and slam home again.

And again.

Each time winding both of us up until we're two tight strings ready to snap.

Sun above, she's made for me. We fit together perfectly, and every moan, every whimper, every hungry kiss brings me to my most centered self.

I'm hers in every sense of the word.

She owns me—body, heart, and soul.

"Blaize," she moans against my mouth. "I'm going to—"

"Yes," I groan over her, upping my pace as I fuck her harder, with long, brutal strokes that have her thighs shaking around my hips.

"Just like that," she says, breathless as her entire body tightens around me. "Right there, Blaize. Oh. My. Stars. Yes." She accentuates every word in time with my thrusts, and fire rips through my veins as her pussy flutters around my cock.

"Fuck," I groan, falling over the edge with her as I spill

inside her.

I move with slow, sweet strokes as I work her down, and she goes limp in my arms.

Carefully, I move us under the water again, cleaning both of us up before leading her out of the water and drying her off. She tries to walk on her own, but her legs are weak in a way that makes me smile with pure, primal pride.

I scoop her up and carry her to our bed, grateful when I find it empty. I'm not above sharing, but tonight, I just want her to myself.

After what happened—from Lock to the traitor to the threat against her life—I just need her.

"I would do that for you too," she says, curling up in my arms.

"What?" I ask, our tones hushed with exhaustion.

She turns in my embrace to look up at me. "If anyone tried to hurt you," she explains. "I would rip them to pieces too."

Warmth ripples down our bond, a reassuring solidarity and unconditional love pulsing down the connection.

"I love you, Blaize," she speaks the words I can feel through our bond, and I run my fingers through her hair as she settles against my chest.

"I love you too, Gessi."

She falls asleep minutes later.

But it's hours before I find solace, because I can't stop the fear from creeping into my veins. Cari must be tortured with worry right now, her mate in the midst of a danger we can't see or stop.

I almost lost my mate tonight, and with the war we're facing, nights like these are numbered.

And I know, without a shadow of a doubt, that I won't survive if anything happens to her.

4

CARI

I shift Lock to his side where he lays in his bed—having moved him to his room so Wynter can check in and monitor him at all hours—wanting to relieve some of the pressure on his back. He doesn't flinch, doesn't moan, nothing. His eyes are still shut, calm except for the random flutter of movement beneath, as if he's dreaming.

I sigh, my body feeling hollowed out.

"You know how angry you'd be with me if I did this to you?" I ask, settling on the other side of the bed to face him. I focus on the anger in order to push through the sadness. "Stars," I continue. "I'd never hear the end of it." I swallow down the tears threatening to burst free again, and force myself to breathe.

Just breathe.

In and out.

In and out.

Lock is breathing. His heart is beating. He's just...lost.

"You would've dove into my mind already and shaken me awake," I say, then huff a sad laugh. "Or spanked, is more like it."

I look over his features, wishing beyond all wishes that his mischievous smirk will shape his lips.

It doesn't.

I trail my fingers over his face, down the line of his jaw.

"Please come back to me," I whisper, closing my eyes and letting one traitorous tear slip free. I know I'm supposed to be strong for him, supposed to keep my mind sharp so I can figure out how to help him, but it's fucking hard when my *mate* is laying here unconscious and I have no idea if I'll ever get him back.

Breathe. Just breathe.

In and out.

In and out.

"Lock—"

"Cari," Steel says from behind me, and I whirl around on the bed. He's standing in the opened doorway, looking much the same as I do—worried, exhausted, hopeless. "Huxton needs us," he says, and I fly off the bed. "Wynter found something."

"I'll be back," I say to Lock before falling into Steel's opened arms, walking in sync with him through the palace.

"Here," he says, holding open a door for me, and guiding me into a room that reminds me a hell of a lot of Talon's labs back home.

A pang of longing hits me in the chest.

I miss Talon.

I miss him and Tor so much it *hurts*. And with Lock...

I feel like I'm being stretched in a hundred different directions, and the connections holding me together are threatening to snap with each passing second.

"Cari," Varian says, wrapping his arms around me in greeting. "We'll figure this out," he says, and I nod against his chest before he releases me.

Gessi sits next to Blaize at a round table that sits off to the left next to a bank of screens and all manner of lab equipment. Blaize flashes me a sympathetic look as Varian joins them. Crane is perched on an upper level of the lab, watching everything from the best vantage point.

Wynter is moving things around in front of the screens, paying us no attention at all, while Huxton sits on the opposite side of the table, features concerned.

Steel pulls out an available chair and I sink into it as he sits to my left.

My pulse quickens the longer we sit waiting for Wynter to turn around and speak to us. I'm about to scream, if only to break the silence, when she finally exhales and turns, jumping at the sight of us.

"Whoa," she says, startled. "When did you all get here?"

I arch a brow at Huxton, silently questioning his assistant's sanity.

"Doesn't matter," she says, waving us off. "This is what you're here for." She waves her hand over the bank of screens, projecting an image onto the space in the center of the round table. It's a pattern of green and purple dots and lines and zigzags I can't even begin to understand. "This is the poison the prisoner tried to attack Gessi with," Wynter explains, and I gape at my best friend.

No one told me.

"I didn't want to bother you while you were with Lock," she says, and guilt clenches my insides. Stars, my best friend was almost poisoned and she was worried it would *bother* me?

"I took care of it," Blaize says with a lethal iciness that sends shivers down my spine.

I have no doubt he did.

"We analyzed it," Wynter continues.

"We?" I ask, glancing at Huxton, but he shakes his head and points to a screen behind Blaize's shoulder.

Talon's face appears, and I bolt out of my seat.

"Talon!" I race over to the screen, tears filling my eyes as I scan his face—his dark eyes, his strong jaw, the goatee he's let get this side of wild.

"Cari," he says, and the relief in his voice has me smiling.

"Little wife!" Tor's voice sounds from behind Talon, who rolls his eyes and shifts, revealing a very shirtless Tor. "I've missed you."

"I miss you both," I say.

"I'm going to kill this general," Tor says without a hint of doubt in his voice. "And then you're coming home to us."

I swallow the rock in my throat. "I can't come home without Lock."

Talon and Tor's gazes turn serious, cracking open my already aching heart. They know something I don't. I can feel it. See it. And I swear the room tilts on its axis as I turn my attention back to Wynter.

"You identified the poison," I say. "Now, tell me you have the cure."

"The poison is eating away at both his body and his power," Talon says behind me.

"You see here," Wynter says, moving her hands outward to zoom in on the image hovering over the table. "The compound is unlike anything we've ever seen before. We've put it through every analytical tool at our disposal..." She pauses, her wide eyes filled with pity.

"Don't," I say shaking my head as I spin back around to the screen showing Talon. "Don't say it, Talon."

He looks wrecked. Purple dusts beneath his eyes, his features looking a haggard in a way I hadn't noticed before. More guilt rises up in a tidal wave. I know my mate. He's a problem solver. That's his gift—his brilliant mind fixes things. And if he looks this bad...

"Talon, please," I beg even as my heart sinks to the pit of my stomach.

"There is no known cure," he says, voice low.

I stumble backward like the words are physical blows until I hit Steel's chest. His arms wrap around me as he guides me back into my chair.

My throat tightens, making it hard to breathe.

Wynter is speaking, saying things I don't understand about science and nature, but the room is spinning.

I fling forward, dipping my head between my legs in an effort to stay grounded.

Steel's powerful hands move up and down my back in soothing strokes that help work a little air into my lungs.

No known cure.

If Talon of all people can't figure out what is killing my mate, then who can? What hope do we have?

Lock. No, not Lock.

"That's not entirely accurate though, is it?" Gessi's voice slices over the roaring in my head, and I blink a few times before looking across the table at her.

"My mother," she says, eyes going distant. "When I was a youngling, she told me stories of a rare, treasured plant that was a source of balance for all things."

"Where are you from?" Wynter asks.

"The Earth Realm, originally," Gessi answers. "The Shattered Isle king took me from my family when I was young, and I've lived as a Shattered Isler ever since." She shakes her head, then focuses. "It was her favorite story to tell—"

"I've heard of this tale," Tor says from the screen behind them. "We're told the story as younglings to foster hope. The All Cure is a fairytale."

"It's not just a story," Gessi argues, and she glances to the side like she's digging deep into the recess of her mind. "My mother showed me the plant. She was the best healer the Earth Realm had before the Shattered Isle king destroyed our village. People would come to our home after being told there was no hope, no *cure*, and she'd heal them. Not with power, but with the plant—the All Cure."

Hope unfurls in my heart. "Where, Gessi?" I ask, barely able to string my thoughts together. "Where is this plant?"

"Wife," Tor says, a plea in his tone. "I fear what will happen if your hopes are raised too high."

I'm on my feet now, determination lacing my blood. I understand Tor's caution—hope is a deadly thing at the best of times. My father taught me that repeatedly while he was alive.

But right now, hope is all I have.

"Can you pull up a map of the All Plane realms from two centuries ago?" Gessi asks.

Wynter immediately complies, waving her hands over her screens before a map replaces the image of poison.

Gessi leans over the table, eyes narrowed as she studies it.

My heart pounds in my chest, adrenaline coursing through my veins and begging me to move.

"Here," she says, pointing to a spot on the map. "This was my village. I don't know where my mother got the plant, but it couldn't have been far from where we lived."

"Shit," Talon hisses.

"What?"

He clicks a few things on his end, and a fresh map lays over the one we stare at.

"This is a current map of the All Plane," he says, high-lighting the spot where Gessi indicated.

"The Stone Realm," I whisper, knowing from experience that the territory is forbidden. My father fled to that location knowing the All Plane princes wouldn't follow. If any one of us steps foot into the territory, it'll be a direct violation of the treaties between us. The Stone Realm has wanted the All Plane to break the peace for years. They'll use any opportunity to fight the All Plane kings.

"The territories changed after the Shattered Isle king attacked," Talon explains. "The previous Earth Realm territory sectioned off and made separate from the Stone Realm."

"I don't care," I say. "I'm going—"

"Wait," Huxton says. "You can't just rush off. We're in the middle of open war."

"I know that—"

"Then you must know that having the general on the throne means more and more people will die. Daily. We have to strategize against him," Huxton says.

Fuck, I know he's right.

I know the general should be our main focus. Saving the people of the Shattered Isle should be our main focus.

But...*Lock.*

I can take out every single person in this room if I had to, if they tried to stop me.

The thought is an intrusive, oily one, but the assassin inside me can't always be tamed.

I take a deep breath, releasing it slowly.

"I'm going with you," Gessi says. "I'm the only one who knows what the plant looks like."

"You're joking!" Huxton shakes his head, his golden eyes blazing. "You are the Shattered Isle queen. You can't leave us to fend for ourselves—"

"I won't be leaving you to fend for yourselves," Gessi

says, sounding more like a queen in that moment than I've ever heard her. A blossom of pride swells in my chest for my best friend. "Luckily, I have four incredibly capable mates."

"You rang?" River says, walking into the room with way more pep in his step than the occasion calls for. His easy smile slips as he takes in the room, his eyes widening. "What did I miss?"

Gessi sighs. "A lot."

"Shit," River mumbles, hurrying to her side. "I'm with her. Whatever she says goes."

If I wasn't so devastated I might laugh at the way he instantly has Gessi's back.

"I too have capable mates," I add, looking to Talon and Tor on the screen, then to Steel who stands at my back. "We will delegate in a way that best serves the Shattered Isle."

Gessi nods in agreement.

"But this is my mate," I say, looking at Huxton, then Wynter, hoping they can understand. "And that bond goes above any royal obligation." I swallow hard. "Gessi and I will go to the Stone Realm and we will bring back the All Cure for Lock. When I have him back, and *only* when I have him back, will I be ready to face the general in open battle."

Huxton blows out a breath, sharing a look with Wynter that I can't quite read.

I pause, noticing how similar they look like Lock and I when we're having silent conversations.

I give Huxton the courtesy of waiting to hear his response, because he's helped save countless lives by taking in refugees of this war, but I don't actually need his permission to go.

"Tor will be on the next ship to the Onyx City," Talon says in full All Plane-king mode. "I'll remain here with Storm to create strategies for the upcoming battles we face.

We can spare some of our armies, and they'll be ready when you call." He's speaking to Huxton, but I know he's speaking on my behalf.

Fuck, I miss him. I need to feel his dominating touch, his ability to take me to places where thoughts and reality don't exist, reducing me to nothing but pleasure and sensation.

"Tor will help train the armies you have and bring the necessities to help secure your city, Huxton," Talon continues. "We're grateful for everything you've done. You will not be left to deal with this alone."

My heart swells in my chest. Tor nods from behind Talon, winking at me before he disappears from view.

Tor. He'll be here soon. He'll be here when I get back. And I know he'll protect Lock with his life until I return with the cure.

"Crane," Gessi calls to her mate without turning around.

Crane leaps over the balcony railing where he'd been perched, landing easily on the floor next to her.

She barely holds back her smile, but I can see a tension between them that is yet to be settled. "You and Blaize will remain here," she says, and Blaize cocks a brow at her from where he sits. "Whatever Huxton needs, I know you'll carry out his requests on my behalf." She glances at River. "You too," she continues. "You can help Wynter in her continued efforts to find an alternative cure in case..." She doesn't finish her sentence, and I'm thankful for it.

"Absolutely," River says. Tor's best friend has a knack for tinkering, much like Talon. It sooths a bit of my broken heart knowing he'll be helping search for a cure on this end too.

"I'm with you, love," Varian says, standing on Gessi's right. "I'll play backup for you and Cari—it'll be like old times again." His smile is wicked and lethal and I have to admit, he'll definitely be an asset going into the Stone Realm.

Steel's hand rests on the small of my back, filling me with a warmth only he can provide. "Me too," he says, and I nod. I wasn't going anywhere without him.

"I can't promise anything," Wynter says, eyes locked on mine. "But I'll do everything in my power to find something."

I can tell from the tight set of her lips she's holding something back. I wave a hand for her to spit it out.

"You don't have much time," she says, sadness weighing her features down.

My stomach plummets. "How much time do I have?"

Her eyes flicker to Huxton's, who dips his head as if to say *she has to know.*

"Best-case scenario," she says, wringing her hands. "Lock has *weeks.*"

My blood runs cold. "And worst case?"

Wynter waves a hand over the images on the table, clearing it. "Five days."

If it weren't for Steel's arm immediately wrapping around my waist, I would've crumpled to the floor.

Five days.

I have five days to find a fairytale cure or Lock dies.

5

GESSI

The smells hit me first—a mix of fresh rain hitting newly upturned soil.

Then the memories.

It's been over a century since the Shattered Isle king tore me from my family, but I can still hear my mother's voice in the back of my mind, can hear the songs she used to sing me, the stories she used to tell. She had a gentle voice, but she could be firm when needed.

I don't remember my father and I never had any siblings—not until Cari. My adopted sister, her father choosing to spare my life and raise me alongside her. Stars, it's like a knife slipping into my chest coming back here. My first home.

What used to be solely the Earth Realm now turned Stone Realm territory, is quiet.

Too quiet.

Our footsteps are light against the green carpet of lush grass that stretches over the wide expanse of valley that tucks up against an outcropping of mountainous rocks, a thick forest bordering the other side.

Something pricks the center of my chest, a dull ache I've done my best to suppress for decades, but being here...it's like I'm six years old again, watching with wonder as my mother concocts potions and elixirs with the magic of her power.

Power that runs through my veins. But I can't create something I've never seen before, never touched. If I can just find the All Cure plant my mother once spoke of, once used, then I'll be able to create as much as we need.

"I don't like this," Varian says as he walks behind me. "It's too quiet."

I nod my agreement, and so do Steel and Cari as they follow behind Varian. We decided it would be best if I lead, just in case we were spotted immediately despite leaving the sky ship in Earth Realm territory. Thankfully, the Earth Realm leader was more than happy to comply but advised us against crossing the border.

An offer of continued peace and a coordinated effort of trade and supplies rests in the pack on my back, signed by all four of the All Plane kings and myself...but there is no one to give it to. No one to barter with in hopes we can explore their land without issue.

We continue our trek, silently and as stealthily as we can. The farther we work our way across the valley, the more my heart aches. Memories flood my consciousness, tearing at the little pieces of my soul that I abandoned years ago. I'd been too young to understand what happened and why I was taken to the Shattered Isle, and once I grew old enough? I'd already fallen in love with the people, with Cari—my sister by choice and bond but not by blood.

My blood had been left here, their corpses long since turned to dust.

I swallow around the lump in my throat as I stop

suddenly, eyes widening at the array of stone homes tucked against the base of the mountain. Moss and vegetation weaves between the creases of the stacked stone, nature taking over what has clearly been abandoned.

The Stone Realm people may have used the homes we vacated when the Shattered Isle king attacked over a century ago, but they haven't been here in months it looks like. The unkempt vines and flowers and poisonous plants surrounding the homes is evidence enough of that.

Cari's fingers interlace with mine as I stop before a home I can't help but recognize. I squeeze her hand, my eyes watery as I look to her. She shouldn't be comforting me. Her mate's life is at stake, and this hurt? My pain? It's an old wound.

"I wish I didn't remember," I admit on a whisper, and she presses her lips together. "I wish I didn't recognize this home."

"It's okay that you do," she says, shaking her head as I lead us inside the stone structure. "I'm sorry for what my father did to you, to your family. For what he—"

"Don't," I say, pulling her close. "You were as young as me. You couldn't have known. Besides, despite everything, I have you now."

Cari sighs, hugging me tight before releasing me. Varian and Steel check the interiors of the abandoned home as I stand in the center of what used to be my mother's work space. It's been changed, the elements of it switched around by whoever took over this space after we were attacked, but I can still see her there, working over a raised, flat stone table as she healed those who came to her for help.

"This place hasn't been lived in for months," Varian says, confirming my earlier suspicions. "I thought Talon said the Stone Realm was teeming with enemies of the All Plane?"

"He did," Cari says, another string of concern lacing her tone.

"Where the hell did they go?" Varian asks, eyeing Steel, who looks just as confused and worried as the rest of us.

"It doesn't matter," I say after a few tense moments. "We're here for one thing and one thing only. If they've abandoned their territory, that's a future problem we'll deal with. For now, we need to search."

Cari nods, following me out of the home. "Do you need more time?" she asks, motioning behind us toward the stone house. "In there," she clarifies. "You can take it, you know. I can't imagine what being back here is doing to you."

I smile softly at her. "I'm okay," I answer honestly. "Whoever the little girl from the Earth Realm was, she's not here any longer." I take a deep breath, relishing the smells surrounding us. "I'm a Shattered Isler. And we're here to help your mate."

Cari squeezes my hand again in solidarity before I lead the way toward the thick bank of trees whose branches stretch and tangle with one another, blotting out most of the sun above us as we pass through the them.

The air is thicker between the tress, the ground uneven as roots lift and twist across the grass. Fallen leaves and flower petals swirl randomly across the ground, fueled by a phantom wind that raises chill bumps along my arms. Mother never let me venture into this forest alone, and even though I'm surrounded by my friends and my mate, I still feel like I'm stepping on forbidden territory.

"Can you describe it to me again, love?" Varian asks, his voice hushed as if he's worried he'll awaken some ancient protector of the trees.

"From what I can remember of the story and what I saw my mother working with, it's a six-petaled flower with bright yellow at the base and fiery red on the tips. It grows on thick vines with sharp, silver barbs, and the petals form an upside-down pyramid shape."

Varian's eyebrows raise as he scans the forest, noting the blankets of neon colors growing up the sides of the trees and around their base. "That shouldn't be hard to find," he says with his classic sarcasm. "Should we split up?"

Steel shakes his head. "Not too far," he says. "I don't want to lose either of you. Especially if we need to get out of here in a hurry."

"I agree," I say, and Varian shrugs.

"Okay," Varian says, pointing behind Steel. "You take that section of land there, stopping before you get to that gnarly tree with all the purple on it."

Steel spots where he indicated and nods.

"And we'll take this section behind us," he says, pointing to another stopping point. "We'll meet back here in the middle to make camp when darkness hits, yeah?"

"Solid plan," Cari says.

"Of course it is," he says. "I made it." He winks at her, but his banter doesn't bring a smile to her lips like it usually does.

She's a shell, and I can't blame her.

I watch her as she and Steel head across the forest, eyes trained on the colorful ground in hopes to spot what we need to save her mate.

I hurry to do the same, praying to all the stars in the sky that I find it.

Because I'm terrified if we don't, we'll not only lose Lock, but Cari too.

∿

"I CAN'T BELIEVE we searched that long and found nothing," I say from where I pace the inside of our tent. Varian and Steel set up camp while Cari and I kept desperately searching as we lost what little light we had when the sun set.

"We will look again tomorrow," Varian says. His forearms are perched on his knees where he sits on a pile of blankets that's to be our bed for the evening. "Harder, longer. The All Cure is legend to most, fairytale to others. The unbelievability surrounding its origins has kept this entire territory from being upturned for centuries. But if it exists, we'll find it."

"It exists," I snap, then cringe. "I'm sorry," I say, dropping to my knees before him.

He smiles at me. "It's all right, love," he says, reaching to draw me against him. "You don't have to be strong in here," he continues, my face in his hands. "It's just me and you."

"I'm fine," I say despite the emotions threatening to spill over.

He cocks a brow at me.

"I'm okay."

"Gess," he says, and the softness in which he says my name breaks me.

I fall against his chest, tears streaming down my cheeks as I sob. His arms encircle me, settling me against his body as I let it all out.

"I can't lose her too," I finally say, sucking in a sharp breath and pulling back enough to look up at Varian.

His brow is furrowed as he wipes away the lingering tears. "Can't lose who?"

"Cari," I say, my breath stuttered as I exhale.

"You're not going to lose her," he assures me, but I shake my head.

"If she loses Lock..." My voice trails off, my mind conjuring too many visuals of what that would do to her.

"She has Steel and Talon and Tor—"

"And I have Blaize and River and Crane, but if I lost you..." A fissure splits down the center of my heart. Losing any one of my mates would be enough to break me. "None of you are replacements for the other," I continue. "You're each vital to my soul."

"You're stronger than that," he says. "Cari is stronger than that. You can't say you'll give up if something happens to any one of us, Gess. With the ongoing war, we can't guarantee the future, let alone tomorrow. And if something happens to me or Crane or Blaize or River, we're going to need you to keep fighting—"

"Don't talk like that," I cut him off. "I'm too emotionally raw to even think about it."

"You brought it up," he chides, that playful smirk shaping his full lips.

I huff a watery laugh, and breathe out another deep sigh.

Varian rubs his hands up and down my back, sparking life back into the hollow spaces inside me. "Cari will be okay. She's a survivor. She always has been."

"I've never seen her like this, though," I say, and he nods. I shudder in his embrace, the mere thought of him being in the same situation as Lock enough to send my body into panic mode.

"Tell me what you need, Gess," he says, holding me tighter. "If you want to go back out there with lanterns and keep searching all night, I will. If you want me to hold you while you let it all out, I will. Just tell me how to help you."

I sigh, focusing on that bond radiating between us, the one pulsing with love and support, passion and friendship.

And suddenly, there is only one way for Varian to help me get through this night.

"Make me forget," I say, looking up at him. "Please, Varian. Make me forget why we're here. Make me forget there is a war brewing that could tear us all apart. Make me forget that my family is buried here."

Varian's eyes gutter, but the raw emotion is quickly replaced by the cockiness I've always been able to count on from him.

"Are you sure, love?" he asks, shifting me on his lap until my spine kisses the pile of blankets we sit on.

"I'm sure," I say, heart racing.

"Then close your eyes." His powerful hands slide up my legs, parting my thighs as he settles between them. "And let me take care of you."

A warm shiver carries down the length of my body as I do as I'm told. I shut my eyes to everything I can't control, submitting entirely to my mate.

I can feel his hands everywhere, all warmth and strength as he strips me until I'm bare to him. And then it's not just his hands I feel, but his *mouth.*

"Varian," I sigh his name as his lips drag down my neck and over my breasts with too-light touches until my nipples are pert and aching for more intensity.

He kisses his way down my stomach, taking his time on my hips, his hands sliding beneath my ass and gripping it hard enough to sting.

I half-hiss, half-moan from the contrast of his gentle kisses and firm grip, but my mind is still torn between the severity of our situation and the present sensations he's creating—

A sharp, brutal bite on my inner thigh has my head eddying and my eyes flying open.

I look down at Varian between my thighs, my chest heaving from the rush of adrenaline spiking my blood from the impact of his teeth on my sensitive flesh. Heat rushes between my thighs as he smirks up at me, his eyes flashing from normal to beastly in the span of a blink.

His tongue slips past his lips, elongated in his powerful form as he licks straight through the heat of me. A moan drags from deep inside my chest as I arch into his carnal kiss, my thigh still stinging from his bite.

"Have I told you how fucking amazing you taste?" he asks, his tongue flicking against my swollen clit with each word.

"Tell me again," I say on a breathy moan, my head falling against the blankets as I arch my hips in a silent plea for more.

"Divine," he groans, flattening his tongue against my throbbing clit before slipping it inside me. "Absolutely *divine*," he says, torturing me some more each time he takes his tongue away to speak.

"Your tongue is divine," I say, fisting the blankets at my side. "More. I need more."

I feel his monstrous smile against my flesh as he wraps his hands around my thighs, spreading me apart for complete access. I can't help but pop up just slightly so I can watch him—

Fuck, his tongue. His eyes. His *body*.

He's somewhere between Varian and beast, the partial shift giving him all kinds of power as he devours me.

I'm completely at his mercy.

And there is no where I'd rather be.

Varian groans as he slips his elongated tongue inside me, curling it in searing strokes that have my entire body clenching with need. His fingers bite into my thighs the heavier I breathe, the more I rock against his mouth, and the pain mixes with pleasure in the sweetest, sharpest way.

Everything in my body narrows to the white-hot knot tightening inside me, the one he's playing with like he has all the time in the world.

"*Varian*," I groan, my voice bordering on a plea.

He smiles again, the beast's eyes meeting mine as he looks up at me from between my thighs. Stars, I almost come from just the sight.

"All right, love," he says, curling his tongue over my throbbing clit.

And then he sucks it into his mouth.

Hard.

My back bows as my orgasm rips through my body, splintering my being into a million little pieces of starlight. I'm spinning, freefalling as my muscles convulse and pulse, the release barreling down my spine so hard and fast I can barely catch my breath.

"Mmm," Varian hums as he rises to his knees between my thighs.

I manage to peel open my eyes, my chest heaving as I look up at him.

Stars, he's glorious—all carved muscle and smooth skin, his power rippling over his body as he holds the partial shift. He licks his lips, moaning at my flavor in a way that makes me wholly liquid.

Gently, he traces his fingers over the bite mark he left on my thigh, the skin there shifting to a darker green than my usual light. It's primal, his branding, and it makes me ache in all the right places.

"Can you handle more, love?" he asks, content to toy with my limp body. "Or do you need a little break?" Challenge flashes in his eyes, and I can't help but grin up at him.

I raise up on my elbows, trailing my fingers down his abdomen until I tease the length of his hard cock. "Give me everything you have, Varian," I say, and his eyes flutter as he rotates his neck.

"You want it all?"

"All," I answer confidently.

I'm fully in this moment with him. We could be in our chambers at home for all my mind knows. There is nothing outside of the need tightening between me and my mate.

A slow, viciously beautiful grin shapes his lips, and my pulse skitters, knowing I have seconds—

He strikes.

Fast, clean, hard.

Pure fucking Varian as his teeth nip at my breast, biting the mound of flesh there until a moan rips from my lips. He kisses the small hurt before curling his tongue over my pert nipple, sucking and worshiping it until it's a peaked bud. He does the same to the other before claiming my mouth in a brutal kiss that steals my breath.

This is life.

This is sustenance.

This is unrestrained joy.

Varian flips me onto my stomach, nudging apart my legs with his knee before situating his cock at my entrance. He drags his head through my slickness, groaning when I wiggle my hips in an effort to get him inside me.

"Varian," I groan when he's content to tease me. "I need you."

"Fuck, Gess," he says, sinking in an inch before pulling back out. "Say it again."

"Please, Varian," I beg, shifting against the blankets in an attempt to relieve the ache between my thighs. "I need you. Now."

"Stars *damn*, mate." He leans over me, his chest pressing against my back as he gathers my wrists in his free hand and pins them above my head, rendering me helpless to his demands. The move turns my blood molten.

He inches his cock inside my heat, slow and torturous until he's seated to the hilt.

I try to move on him, but he has me completely, utterly pinned.

Varian holds us there, motionless save for my throbbing pussy and our ragged breaths. He drags his nose along the line of my jaw before reaching my ear. "You're mine," he breathes the words, and searing shivers dance over my skin.

He pulls all the way out only to slam home again, and I see fucking stars.

His grip is brutal on my wrists, his body flush atop mine. He's consuming as he pounds into me from behind, bottoming out each time. There is nothing but him and the way he's using my body to make us both feel good.

And I'll never, ever get enough.

A moan escapes my lips as he bites my neck at the same time he bottoms out, my entire body clenching around him as he fucks me so hard I can't think around the way he feels.

Fire.

He's pure fire and a little bit monster and one hundred percent mine.

He pulls up enough to slap his hand across my ass, the sensation rocketing through my body and making me even more slick. I rock against him with the freedom, pushing back against him as he plunges into me.

"Fucking perfect," he groans, smoothing his hand over my still stinging flesh. "Your skin darkens so beautifully for me."

"*Stars*, Varian," I say, trembling as he thrusts into me again and again. "Do you see what you do to me?"

A low growl rumbles his chest, and he slips a hand beneath my hip, rolling his fingers across my over-sensitive clit. His lips are back at my ear, his thrusts as relentless as his fingers. "I see you," he says, the words more powerful and sincere than the teasing from earlier. "I see all of you, Gess," he continues, speaking over my moaning as he continues to rub against my clit. "And I love every fucking piece of you."

He slams into me harder, like he's trying to further brand himself on my soul, all while he pinches my clit until I clench around him, another orgasm crashing around me in a wave so fierce I'm swept totally away.

Blinding pleasure snaps through my mind, my body, as I convulse around him, my thighs so slick he glides in and out with a speed and ease only his power can manage before he spills inside me.

Slowly, he works us both down, until we're hot and sated and I can barely move when he shifts to clean us both up. After, he settles down beside me, dragging me half on his chest as we lay in silence, catching our breath and slipping into a seductive sleep that I know I'll never be able to properly thank him for enough.

6

CARI

"**C**an you see anything?" I call up to Steel, who has scaled a massive tree in order to cover more ground in our search.

"Shit," Steel hisses from above, his eyes narrowed on something to the west.

"What is it?" Gessi asks, a strain in her voice as she exits her tent, Varian right behind her.

Dawn just broke over the sky, little beams of buttery sunlight penetrating the small cracks in the thick forest canopy.

Steel moves down the tree with a speed and grace only he can manage, and his blue eyes are severe as he hits the ground. "There are massive buildings to the west," he explains. "They look vacant, but I know weapons production when I see it."

"Shit," I echo Steel's earlier sentiment. "So, Lock was right," I continue. "The general was gathering resources." I shake my head. "Expendable resources. The Stone Realm."

Steel nods, and our little group goes silent for a few moments.

One problem at a time.

I take a deep breath. "Any sign of the plant?"

Steel presses his lips together before he shakes his head. I can feel the disappointment radiating down our bond, but it does little to shake my resolve. I have to find this cure. I *will find it.*

"I had a dream last night," Gessi blurts, drawing our attention.

"You were able to sleep?" I ask, grateful she was able to get some rest. I hadn't been able to, and as a result, neither did Steel.

"Oh, yes," Varian answers for her. "The queen slept very hard."

Steel covers his laugh with a cough, and I can feel the joke, feel the reaction I'm supposed to have, but it doesn't reach the surface. It bounces off the shield of worry and doubt and sheer terror that coats everything inside me right now.

Gessi can barely hide her smile, and I can't blame her. Being with your mate is like nothing else in this world. She should be enjoying the new love they have between them.

"Yes," she continues. "I think coming back here jarred loose some old memories I've kept buried." She glances around, expertly scanning the area before heading south.

We all hurry to follow her, Varian on her heels.

"What was your dream about?" I ask as we continue to weave through the thicket of trees.

"My mother," she says without looking back. "She took me here once," she explains, moving left.

She touches the tree trunks she passes, pausing for a few seconds with her eyes closed. I've seen her do it before—use her powers to communicate with the land. It's not an exact science, but I'm praying to the stars that whatever she's doing will help us find what we came for.

"I can see it," she continues. "The day she took me out here, she was collecting the All Cure plant. She once told me there were only certain beings who could find it, who could wield it. Beings like her. Like me."

My heart stutters at her words, treacherous hope flooding my over-exhausted system.

"That would explain why this territory hasn't been searched over for centuries," Varian says. "That and no one fully believes it's more than a fairytale. Except us," he adds the last part quickly.

"They grew in a tight cluster," Gessi continues. "But there were *hundreds* of them." She moves faster now, not pausing at the tree trunks.

I move in sync with her, heart racing.

This is it.

We're going to find the cure and get it back to Lock with time to spare.

He's going to be okay.

"It should be right around here," Gessi calls, taking a hard right past a grove of trees that are so twisted and gnarled together we have to climb over their massive roots to follow her. "It should be—"

Gessi stops abruptly as we clear the roots of the trees, the move depositing us in a little meadow encircled by the thick trees. It looks so unnatural it could've been strategically planted centuries ago. The grass is a vibrant green and yellow, but there is a giant patch of upturned earth in the middle that is black as midnight.

"*No,*" Gessi breathes the word, and my heart plummets to my stomach as she drops to her knees in front of the dark earth. She digs her fingers into the soil, slamming her eyes shut. Two tears roll down her cheeks as she shakes her head. "It's like someone came and ripped it all out by the roots."

Everything slows down, even the sound of her voice.

She sounds very far away, and I'm shaking.

My entire body is *shaking*.

"It's gone," she says, devastation coloring her tone. "It's all gone."

I can't breathe. My heart is racing so hard my throat threatens to close and all I can see is Lock, unconscious in that bed as the poison slowly eats away at him.

"No," I whisper the word, shaking my head. Rage rising in a swell of pressure inside me.

Not him. Not Lock.

I've failed him.

I've *failed* him.

I want to kill the person who injected him despite knowing he's already dead.

I want to rip out the hearts of *everyone* who supports the general, everyone who is on the wrong side of this war.

I want to maim and kill and shred.

I want Lock. I want him *back*.

"Cari," Steel calls to me, but his voice barely breaks through the storm brewing inside me.

"No!" The word breaks through me in a scream, scraping against my tight throat as I roar at the world. My power builds, trembling with pressure as it spills out of me, coating the lush grass around me in frost.

"Cari." Steel's arms are around me as he hauls me against him, but I shake him off, not wanting to hurt him. I can't control the rage pouring out of me, I can't stop the grief from consuming every inch of me—

"By order of the king of the Shattered Isle, on your

knees!" a gruff, masculine voice splinters the storm inside me, and I snap to the present.

"Fuck," Varian says as he positions himself in front of Gessi.

There are two dozen Stone Realm people wearing the general's new uniforms surrounding us along the borders of the circle of trees. They each have a weapon trained on us, a sleek blaster with their insignia on it—no doubt the general now has hundreds of these weapons in his possession if Steel's assumptions about the weapons development is correct. This is who's been supplying the general. This is why there is barely anyone here—they Stone Realm people are likely at the Shattered Isle palace, serving the general.

"On your knees," the guard says again. "You've trespassed on what will soon be the new capital of the All Plane, ruled by our Shattered Isle king. Submit or die."

Gessi glances back at me, looking fully prepared to drop to her knees.

We *are* heavily outnumbered.

We're at a disadvantage.

Kneeling would be the right play here. Submit now and fight later.

But these people, they work for *him*.

They work for the man who took my mate away from me.

I give Gess a nod, and she slowly goes to her knees. Then Varian.

The sight makes my stomach churn with acid.

Steel stands behind me, unmoving.

And I can't help but stare at that patch of dark earth, stare at what would've been Lock's salvation.

I snap my eyes to the people surrounding us.

They did this.

They took it.

And I will not kneel for them.

"Now, bitch," the guard says, stomping across the distance until his blaster touches my chest.

Steel growls, stepping forward, but I raise a hand to stop him.

My lip curls slightly as I glare up at the guard. "I only kneel for my mates."

Ice *explodes* out of me.

Needle-sharp spears that fly in all directions so fast Steel barely has time to duck.

Sounds of tearing flesh and gushing wounds fill the air, quickly followed by the dropping of two dozen bodies.

The guard in front of me still has that smug expression on his face—now permanently frozen—as he falls before me, a spear of ice sunk straight through his heart.

Varian and Gessi are on their feet and moving toward me in seconds, but Steel urges them back as another scream tears through me.

I drop to my knees, my entire being crying out for Lock as I stare at that fucking hollow piece of earth where his cure should be.

"I've lost him," I cry, rocking back and forth as I try to get a hold of my power. It's a chaotic, angry thing as it spills from me—barbs of ice flying in all directions, frost coating everything in my eyesight. "I've lost him," I say again, my tears freezing on my cheeks before they can fully fall.

Steel drops to his knees before me, filling my line of sight with nothing but his face, his piercing blue eyes. A frosty gust of wind kisses his cheeks and snowflakes slide over his shirt as he cups my face.

"*Steel*," I choke out his name through my sobs. "I've lost him."

"Cari, I need you to breathe."

"I can't." I try to breathe through the onslaught of power escaping my body, try to breathe around the heartbreak tearing through me and I *can't*.

"You can," Steel says with pure determination.

"Run," I grind out the word, my chest heaving as I try to catch a breath. "Steel, you need to *run*."

His skin is turning blue from the cold, from my power lashing out at everything around me.

"Never," he says, his warm breath a puff of steam in the cold as he draws me closer. "I'll never run from you, mate."

Mate.

Mate.

I fall against his chest, shaking in his powerful embrace as the word clangs through me.

Steel is my mate.

And Talon.

And Tor.

And...

"I'm here," Steel says into my ear before his lips press against my cheek. "I'm right here. I'm with you. Now, *breathe*."

His command slides through the shields of power shuddering all around me. It weaves its way past my panic, past my grief, inching in just enough that my lungs open and I draw in one breath.

Then two.

"Good," he says, shifting so he can look down at my face. He presses his lips against mine, the kiss searing with heat that clears my racing mind. "Again," he says.

I breathe. Over and over again until my power trickles out of my veins, settling beneath my skin in a raw sort of way, as if it's grieving along with me.

I fist Steel's shirt, shaking my head against his chest before I look up at him. "I failed," I say. "I failed him."

Steel shakes his head, waving at someone behind me to get back.

I glance over my shoulder, noting the shocked and scared look on Gessi's face as she tries to come to me.

Varian holds her back, scooping her over his shoulder as he shifts into the monster beneath his skin before bounding out of the circle of trees. Running away from me. Like they should.

Like Steel should've.

The entire meadow is now a frozen circle of ice, the trees coated in thick icicles that jut in all directions like the deadliest trap.

Me.

I did that.

"I could've killed one of you," I say, turning back to Steel.

"You didn't," he says, then kisses me again.

And again.

He kisses me like we're at home after a training session, teasing each other on our way to the bathing chamber.

He kisses me like I'm still the mate he loves, like I'm not the monster my father raised me to be.

He kisses me like I didn't just fail him, fail his brothers.

Like I didn't just lose Lock for all of us.

My tears fall freely now, and he kisses those away too.

"I love you," he says against my mouth before drawing away to simply hold me as I cry. "I will always love you."

And I cling to him, to the bond between us, to his words as I try to stop myself from shattering completely.

7

STEEL

"**B**rother," Tor says as we make it back to Huxton's palace. He wraps me in a tight hug, and I return the sentiment. "Where is my little wife?" he asks, looking behind me like she might appear at any second.

"I gave her something to help her sleep," I explain. We returned only an hour ago, emptyhanded. Both Gessi and Cari had barely spoken on the return trip, and the more I watched Cari turn inward, the more my mounting terror grew. She gladly accepted the sleep tonic I offered, taking it quickly before curling up in bed next to Lock.

His condition hasn't changed, which is both a blessing and a curse. He hasn't worsened, to Wynter's surprise, but he hasn't improved either, no matter how many remedies she tries.

"Ah," Tor says, clapping me on the shoulder before moving out of the way.

Talon is the next to meet us in the hallway, hugging me just as fiercely. With one of our brothers down, it's easy to see how much we take for granted.

And Cari...Sun, I've never seen her like this before.

Never seen her lose control of her powers like that before.

And I understand why. I understand the strain this is putting on her. Losing a brother would be devastating, but losing her? Losing my mate? I don't know how any of us would survive it. It would be like having a chunk of my heart ripped from my chest.

"How is Storm fairing?" I ask Talon as I release him.

"Holding strong," Talon answers, motioning to me and Tor to follow him.

We head into what has clearly been deemed a makeshift workshop for him here in Huxton's palace. I honestly don't know how we're ever going to repay the generous leader of this city, but I plan to do everything in my power to.

Talon hits a few buttons on one of his work stations, and Storm's face fills a screen on the wall.

"How is our queen?" he immediately asks.

Blaize had done the same the second we returned—it's reassuring to know our friends love her too and are just as worried as we are.

"Sleeping," I say, and leave it at that. No one outside of our little group needs to know about her loss of control in the Stone Realm. Not that Storm would judge her—they've become close since she became queen—but this form of communication could easily be intercepted. Better to keep those details to ourselves until we can speak safely in person.

Storm nods, then shifts to business mode, relaying all situations in the All Plane as he acts as king regent in our absence. It's a lot for Talon to ask of his best friend, but the male was born for leadership. We're lucky to have him on our side.

The reports from Storm take a full three hours with a

whole lot of back and forth on what we're to do about this war—all in a code so as to not be intercepted by the general — especially now that we know the Stone Realm has not only chosen a side, but has been preparing for this long before we knew about it.

"I've already started making the preparations we spoke about, Talon," Storm says. "The people have started rationing supplies and plans have been distributed should we need to evacuate the surrounding cities within the palace's stronghold."

"Good work," Talon says, rubbing his forehead where he sits in a chair across the room.

Tor has taken up pacing the length of the room on the opposite side, whereas I feel like I'm melting into the chair I sit in. It's been a long fucking week, to say the least, and I still feel like I'm not doing enough.

"Have we determined how much of our armies we can spare?" Talon asks.

Storm nods.

"Are we strategizing?" Gessi asks as she comes into the room. She scans the area, searching for Cari, but I merely shake my head when she flashes me a questioning glance.

"You should've called us in here sooner," Varian says from behind her, falling into a seat next to her after she sits.

"Anyone else I can interrogate for you?" Blaize asks as he comes into the room, River right behind him. They all surround their mate, their queen, in a unified front that makes me prickle with unmerited jealously.

Cari deserves all of us at our strongest, and we're barely holding it together.

"We just started to get to the heart of this plan," Talon says, an edge to his tone.

"Go on then," Varian says, waving a hand at Storm.

"We can spare forty percent of the All Plane armies," Storm explains, "and still have enough of a military presence to hopefully ward off direct attacks."

"Hopefully," Cari's voice jars me. I move to get up from my seat, but she waves me off as she walks into the room, giving Talon and Tor a weak smile as she sits between me and Gessi. "There is little hope to go around, Storm."

Tor comes behind Cari, sliding his hands along her shoulders in a silent greeting whereas Talon simply shares a look with her I can barely understand. Their relationship has always been different than ours, but the love there is undeniable.

Gessi slides her hand into Cari's, a show of silent support that endears me even more to her best friend.

"Hope is a fickle thing," Storm says, speaking in a friendly tone that he adapts whenever he and Cari are together. "You know that better than anyone. But, in some cases, like war times, it's a valuable commodity. I'm not going to skimp on it now."

Cari nods. "How are you faring?"

"I'm king regent," he says, puffing out his chest. "I'm the best I've ever been."

A huff that somewhat resembles a laugh comes from my mate, and I breathe a little easier. We can all clearly tell Storm is lying—he's carrying the weight of an entire kingdom on his shoulders. It doesn't matter how fast he is, he can't outrun the responsibility we placed upon him. But he's trying for Cari, and I love him for it.

"So, forty percent," Cari says, nodding. "When will they arrive?"

"Within the week," Storm answers, back to business.

"Good," she says, and I can see the edge of rage in her eyes. It hasn't fully left since the Stone Realm and I'm not sure if it ever will. If the worst should happen and we do lose Lock, I'm not sure if my mate will ever fully be whole again, and that *terrifies* me.

"I'd like to move—"

Storm's words are cut off as his image freezes on the screen.

Talon sits up straighter in his chair, clicking a few things at his work station. "Fuck me," he snaps as he frantically works at the station.

"What is it?" Cari asks.

"It's a transmission," he says as the screen shifts from Storm's face to...

Fucking hell.

Gessi and Cari are both on their feet, drawing closer to the screen like that will help them understand what they're seeing.

"That's the Shattered Isle royal square," Gessi says, breathless.

"There," Cari says, pointing when she spots him.

The general.

He's wearing a twisted crown of black stone and diamonds as he stands in the middle of a wide dais, looking down on a crowd of people. Some are bowing, but others are defiant and being forced to watch by the general's guards.

The general looks directly into the camera, his eyes cold. He knows what he's doing.

We're all on our feet now.

"There are those of you who still cling to the past," the general says, his voice booming over the now silent crowd. "Those of you who are having trouble...adjusting to the new order." His smile is malicious as he looks to the camera again before giving a single wave with those spindly fingers

of his. "This should help those of you who are still struggling along."

A handful of guards climb the dais, each one dragging a
struggling Shattered Isle citizen, bound in chains.

"Oh, stars," Gessi gasps, her hand flying over her lips.

"They're all..." Cari's hands are fists at her sides, and the
room goes a few degrees cooler. "They're all wearing our
symbols," she finally finishes.

The prisoners who are now centered on the dais in a row
of six each have something that represents Cari or Gessi on
their person. A shirt with our All Plane insignia or a tattoo
of a flower that represents Gessi's rule.

"These people were graciously given the opportunity to
renounce their previous loyalties," the general says, pacing
before them. "They declined my generous offer."

He glances at the camera once more, and Cari's entire
body starts to shake. I smooth my hand around her hip,
drawing her close. Tor is on my right, running his hand
down her arm too.

"Their mistake." The general flicks his wrist, and a long,
skinny blade drops from inside the cuff of his jacket. The
crowd gasps, but he doesn't hesitate to drag the blade along
each prisoner's throat as he walks by them.

"No!" Cari yells as the horrific scene plays out for us—
blood splashing upon the dais, screams of terror ringing out
from the crowd as the bodies drop. "No," she whispers, her
arms wrapping around her stomach as she doubles over,
turning away from the screen.

Gessi is crying, shaking her head as shock colors her
features. She can't tear her eyes away from the screen.

"Let my kindness be a lesson," the general says to the
crowd. "You will renounce the traitorous queens or you will
die."

I rub my hands up and down Cari's back as she tries to regain her composure.

"And for those particular false queens," the general continues, the words snapping Cari to attention. She returns her gaze to the screen, ice splintering its way over the floor beneath her feet. "If you come here and submit yourselves, I'll accept your blood as payment for all their lives."

River is holding Gessi, who looks on the brink of collapse, but Cari's spine straightens.

"Until you do," he continues. "All their blood is on your hands."

The transmission cuts to black before Storm's face returns in a confused state.

"What in the sun happened?" Storm asks.

"Storm," Cari says, her voice absolutely lethal.

"Yes?"

"You need to send the armies. Send them now."

He blinks a few times, looking to Talon for confirmation, even though he doesn't need Talon's approval.

"Your queen just gave you an order," Talon says by way of answer. "Get it done."

"I'm on it," he says, then ends the transmission, the screen going black.

IT'S another few hours before we all settle on some form of a plan—it's not solid, but it's all we have for now.

We have to wait on the armies to arrive and continue training the Onyx City soldiers here. And as much as my mate wants to rush into battle—understandably—we can't. We'd lose. On some level, I know she knows that. Cari is one of the most brilliant people I know, but she can't see past her rage right now. It's up to us to help center her so we don't lose her too.

We haven't lost him yet, I chide myself, but I can't help it. My hope is dwindling the longer it goes without Lock waking up, without him fighting this.

He's the strongest of us, not that we've ever told him that. But we all know it. Hell, the general knew it, that's why he targeted him first. Lock is the most powerful being across the realms, and if he can't break out of this, what chance do the rest of us have if we're attacked with the same poison?

And I thought the concoction the general fashioned that stripped us of our powers was bad. This is worse, so much worse.

The general will die.

But it has to be at the right time. When we have the most advantage, and from what I know of my mate, she'll be the first to rush off in the night to handle it herself if we don't keep an eye on her.

"Did you eat?" I ask as I walk into my bedchamber, finding Cari perched cross-legged on my bed. I asked her to stay with me in my chambers tonight.

"A little," she answers. She's wearing a simple pair of black cotton pajamas, but she looks so frail sitting there with her head down, shoulders drooped as if a strong gust of wind would knock her right off the bed.

I know she's anything but frail. She's deadly, strong, and beautiful, but I hate seeing her this way. There isn't anything I can do or say to make this situation right. Words of comfort will only be patronizing and any promise I might try and make her will be empty.

The only thing I can do is be with her.

Sit with her in this shared pain.

Talon and Tor are still busying themselves with strategy

and war preparation, or they'd be here too. They'll get their time with her soon, I know it, and choosing between her and what needs to be done is killing them.

But our mate is not alone.

I hurry out of my clothes, slipping on a pair of loose shorts before I climb onto the bed next to her. She melts into my arms when I reach for her, and I sigh at the contact of her body against mine. I shift to lean against the ornate headboard, the sleek black cushioning comforting as I hold her tight.

She's cold. Colder than her usual temperature, like her powers are in control instead of her.

I reach around us, gathering the blankets around her before holding her again, trying to somehow work my heat and love into her body.

"I'm sorry," she whispers after a while, her cheek pressed against my chest.

I shift my head, looking down at her. "What for?"

"For what happened in the Stone Realm," she says, dark eyes locked on mine as she reaches up and traces a finger over my cheek, right where her ice had stung my skin.

I hold her hand there, leaning into the cool touch. "I'm okay," I say. "You have nothing to be sorry for."

She sighs. "I have a lot to be sorry for."

I furrow my brow, scanning her face. Her full lips are turned down in what has become a nearly constant exhaustion, her smooth blue skin leached of color in some areas, as if her power or this grief is sucking the life from her.

"Lock isn't my only mate," she continues, and I nod with realization. "I have you," she says, snuggling closer. "I have Tor and Talon. I'm luckier than anyone across the realms to have the mates I do. But..." She hesitates, indecision in her eyes.

I move beneath her, situating her until one leg is on either side of my hips, our chests flush so she can't look away as I cup her cheeks. "Tell me," I encourage her.

"Every day he doesn't wake up I feel like I'm losing a piece of myself," she admits. "I feel like I can't breathe. I feel like we're both drowning and he's so close but I can't reach him." Tears well in her eyes. "All I want to do is crumble, to take more of that sleeping tonic and numb myself to the pain that's eating away at me." She shakes her head. "But I can't do that. I can't let myself break because war is here and I have to *fight*. He's already won in that way," she continues. "Taking away my ability to find a solution or to grieve."

"He's not won," I say, swiping away her tears with my thumbs. "Look at me, Cari," I say when her eyes fall. "You *can* break. You can crumble with me and I'll be right here to put you back together when you're done."

A little of her light comes back to her eyes, love and compassion radiating down our shared bond. I breathe in the sensation before slanting my mouth over hers in a gentle kiss. I'm not trying to seduce her, not right now. That's not what she needs, but when she does I'll be here.

Right now, she needs to fall apart in a different way.

Needs to be *allowed* to fall apart. To not have to be the strong one, the assassin queen with the weight of this war on her shoulders. She needs to have the safety and the space to let it all out.

"Let go," I say, kissing her again before wrapping my arms around her until she settles her head over my shoulder. I can feel her heart beating against my chest, can feel her breaths lengthening the longer I hold her. "Let it all go, wife. Whatever you need to feel, *feel* it. I'll hold you through it all and when you're done, we'll figure out a way to win this war and save Lock...together."

There. At least those aren't empty promises, because we will figure this out, one way or another. The results? They can vary, but I'll do whatever I have to. We all will.

Sobs wrack her body.

I stroke her back through the throes of it.

Cries turn into angry, wordless pleas.

I run my fingers through her long black hair, never flinching from the ice that pricks my skin as she releases all she's kept pent up.

After a while, she goes silent, her breathing matching mine in long, deep heaves, and I feel her muscles relax against me.

"Thank you," she whispers.

"For what?"

"For letting me break."

I swallow around a rock in my throat, wishing I could do more, wishing I could fix this for her. I kiss the top of her head, feeling her grow heavier against me as her body succumbs to the exhaustion wreaking havoc upon it.

"Always," I whisper as I send all the power I can down our bond, hoping it fills those empty spaces inside her with strength enough to rest.

8

CARI

I throw ice dagger after ice dagger at the wooden target across the room, each tip sinking into my mark, but it brings me no relief.

No satisfaction at a job well done.

No gratification for honing my skills.

Nothing.

Anger and restlessness rub the inside of my skin, making me feel like I'll explode at any moment.

At least I have my powers in control, that is something to be grateful for.

For now.

What happened in the Stone Realm...

They deserved it, but I hate the line I'm walking since Lock fell unconscious—I'm teetering on the edge of losing myself completely. Of relying on the deadly assassin inside me to creep up and take over, make everything better by taking everything away.

Snick, snick, snick.

Ice daggers fly toward more targets pressed against the farthest wall of the training room, each hitting their mark.

I imagine the general's face on each one. Imagine my blades sinking into his skull instead of the wood before me.

"Your aim is still absolute shit." Varian's voice fills the space behind me, the bastard sneaking up on me. I whirl, releasing another dagger—

He catches it with a partially shifted hand, cocking a brow at me. "Saw that move before you even thought to make it."

A raw, hoarse laugh rips out of me. He's still an insufferable bastard.

I've missed my friend.

And he's not wrong. We've trained together our whole lives in the most brutal of ways—the general and my father forcing him to shift into the beast beneath his skin and attack me until I learned how to fend him off.

He flings the dagger my direction, but I don't move as it flies right past my face, the cool air kissing my cheek before it sinks into the target behind me.

"Did Gessi send you?" I ask, turning back around to throw more daggers.

"No," he says, sounding offended. "You know, just because she's my mate doesn't mean I do everything she says."

Another laugh comes, shocking the hell out of me. I haven't laughed in days. Not like this. I glance over my shoulder, eying him.

He shrugs. "Okay, maybe I do, but she didn't send me," he says. "Crane is with her."

"How is that going?" I ask, genuinely curious. Things have been on uneven ground with them since they found out they were mates, and he's been trying to earn back her trust for past grievances every day.

In her eyes, he already has it, but he's a glutton for punishment, and always has been.

"About as well as you'd expect," Varian says, now standing at my right, sizing up every throw I make like we're younglings again and he's coaching me on aim. "Crane is stubborn, but he's coming around. I bet they'll fully make amends soon."

I nod, hope pulsing faintly in my heart for the pair. "They better do it fast," I say, chucking another dagger. "You never know when..." I stop myself from speaking the rest of the words out loud.

You never know when it'll be your last day together.

"Oh, nah," Varian says, sucking his teeth at me. "I didn't realize we were having a feel sorry for ourselves party," he says. "I would've brought wine."

I glare at him. "I'm not—"

"You are," he cuts me off. "And fine, fair enough." He steps in front of me, eyes narrowed as he looks down at me. "But *really*, Cari?"

"Really, what?" I ask, adrenaline and anger sizzling together in my blood.

"Oh, nothing, just wondering when you'll remove your head from your ass."

I gape at him before shoving against his massive chest. "Asshole."

He laughs, shaking his head. "I'm not the asshole, you are." He partially shifts, his beastlike hands extending to shove me back.

"What in the *stars*, Varian?"

"You're giving up," he fires at me.

I take a swing at him and miss as he dances out of the way. "I am not."

"You are," he says, his eyes flickering totally black as he

shifts into his beast form another inch. "I can see it all over your face. You're letting what's happened to Lock consume you—"

"What would you do?" I fire back, landing a punch across his jaw.

Obsidian ripples along his body as he fully shifts, his size growing to four times mine.

"That's it," he says, his voice garbled from the shift as he speaks through his razor-sharp teeth. He waves me over in a challenge. "Give me your best, Cari."

"Answer me," I snap, rushing him. He dodges each of my attacks, the jerk.

"Land another hit and I will."

We could be younglings again, sparring in the Shattered Isle dungeons during the daylight hours when the general and my father thinks we're sleeping. Varian trained me in secret, hating that they forced us to fight but wanting us both to get so good at it we could do it without really harming each other.

I chase him around the room, hating that his shifted form gives him all the speed and strength I could only ever dream of possessing. He'd even be able to hold his own with Steel, if they ever fought. What I wouldn't do for an ounce of Steel's speed so I could catch him now—

He darts left, but I anticipate his retreat, cutting him off with a crack across his jaw that barely phases him.

"If it were Gess," he says, answering like he promised. "I'd be a mess," he admits right before he backhands me so hard, I stumble across the matted floor.

The pain shakes something loose inside me, a presence that hasn't been able to reach me in days. "Then why are you giving me hell?"

I charge him, swiping his feet out from under him,

smiling at the sound of his back hitting the mat. The wind whooshes out of his lungs as I loom over him, and he points up at me with his elongated, obsidian finger.

"That," he says, leaping to his feet as he continues to point at me. "That right there is why I'm giving you hell."

I furrow my brow for a second before I realize he's pointing at my smile.

I'm smiling.

Beating Varian has always made me smile because it's so fucking hard to do. Plus, every time I won, my father and the general would reward us with a break.

I huff, shaking my head before barely dodging another swing from him. Of course, he wouldn't pat me on the back and tell me everything was going to be okay, he's not that kind of friend. Stars, he's more like the grumbly older brother I never had.

"Your core is shit," he lobs at me. "I thought you were training every day with Tor and Steel?"

"I do," I groan, swinging and missing again.

"It's cute that they think what they're doing is training," he says, sweeping my legs.

My spine smacks against the mat, blurring my vision for a second before I jump to my feet again. "Their training is perfect," I growl.

"Ha!" He backflips away from an ice sword I conjure. "They've clearly been taking it easy on you."

I roll my eyes.

"Where is the Cari who wouldn't stop until I bled? Where is the deadly assassin who would never let anyone tell her what to do? Where is—"

I drop to a knee, smacking my palms against the mat, ice spiderwebbing its way across the surface until he slips. He crashes against the mat, the momentum sending him sliding right toward my awaiting, icy fingers.

I wrap them around his thick, beastly throat. "I win," I say, breathless.

Varian's oversized smile shapes his shifted lips, revealing all those gleaming sharp teeth. "There she is," he says, right before he elbows my forearm so hard I instantly release his throat. He kicks out at me, and I land on my back beside him.

We both look at each other from where we lay on our backs on the mat, and laugh.

It's a cleansing, soothing sort of laugh that somehow scrapes away the sticky hopelessness clinging to me, and it feels so good and so wrong at the same time that I start to cry again.

I'm so fucking tired of crying.

"Fuck," Varian sighs, shaking his head.

Neither one of us move to get up, we just lay there, with me crying and him sighing.

"Chin up," he says, smacking my arm, instantly stopping my tears. "Lock is the scariest motherfucker I know," he continues, releasing his shift until he's just Varian again. Teal eyes meet mine instead of black when I turn my head to look at him. "He'll beat this on his own. I know it."

"How do you know?" I ask, chest still heaving from the fight. Lock and him have been friendly since the day they met, but still...I know Lock better than anyone and I'm terrified.

"Because I'm not his mate," he says, rolling his eyes. "You can't see past losing him, and I get that, but Lock *will* beat this. You have to know that. Someone with that amount of power? They don't bow out easily."

I roll my head back, staring at the training room ceiling.

Hope slivers into the hollow spaces of my heart.

Varian is right.

I want him to be right.

But I can't shake the anger, the rage, the fear.

After a few moments, I decide to change the subject. "What are the odds the general took the All Cure when he took possession of the Stone Realm?"

"High," Varian answers. "If he has someone working for him that could find it and wield it, he wouldn't hesitate to take it all. You know his obsession with poisons. What better way to concoct one than by studying something like the All Cure?"

Ice bites my palms as my anger mounts. "I'm going to kill him, slowly."

"You'll have to fight me," Varian says, cocking a brow at me. "Cause I'm killing him first."

I laugh again, and Varian pops up, offering me a hand. I take it, and he helps haul me to my feet.

"I needed this," I say, clapping his muscled shoulder.

"I know," he says, the understanding in his eyes, in his voice, is void of his usual cocky banter. "We're all here," he continues. "And you know I've always got your back."

I nod, knowing he always has. Every time it counted back home, he never faltered. He's a good friend, a better brother.

"Now, let's stop this feeling sorry shit," he says, shaking off the serious mood. "Drop and give me twenty."

"Screw you, Varian," I say, throwing another punch instead.

He shifts before I can make the connection.

∾

MY BODY FEELS BEATEN and worked to all hell as I stand under the hot stream of water in the shower, but for the first time since Lock went down...I feel more like myself.

Maybe it's because Varian didn't treat me like I was going to break at any second or maybe it's because he has unflinching faith that Lock will be okay. Either way, I don't stand under the water and cry like I have been the last few nights, and that feels like a win.

I dry off, then wrap a luxurious towel around my body, breathing deeply with a sigh of satisfaction at the stillness inside me. I know it won't last long, but I'm filled with gratitude for the friends I have who support me. And I have my mates...I don't know how I got so lucky.

A spear of terror slices down the middle of me.

What if I'm too lucky?

What if one person isn't supposed to possess so much wealth in love?

What if what's happened to Lock is the price for all the love surrounding me?

The intrusive *what if's* swarm my mind, threatening to steal every ounce of solidity I've managed to grasp today.

Lock isn't some celestial bargaining chip. The stars did not damn me or him. What's happening is directly linked to the general and his heartless, evil soul.

And I'm going to fucking slaughter him.

"You were in there a long time, little wife." Tor's voice startles me as I pad barefoot into my bedchamber. "I was just about to come in there and drag you out," he continues, and I finally spot him sitting in the dark, in a chair tucked in the corner of my room. "Or join you." He shrugs. "Whichever you preferred."

A smile shapes my lips, my heart soaring at the sight of him. It's been too long since I've seen him. Sure, I saw him in passing during the businesses of the last two days, but there was no quality in our time.

"*Mate*," I say, something loosening in my chest a little.

Tor is out of the chair in seconds, scooping me up into his arms and slanting his mouth over mine.

There is nothing gentle in the kiss, no timid check to see if I'm emotionally intact, not with Tor. He'll never treat me like glass, and right now? That's exactly what I need.

I gasp at the contact, my mind whirling as he slides his tongue into my mouth, reexploring every inch until I wrap my legs around his waist. The towel covering me shifts downward, and Tor makes quick work of slipping it off and tossing it across the room.

He draws back enough to look at me. "I've missed you," he says, voice ragged.

"So much," I agree, kissing him again.

He groans, palming my ass with a squeeze that makes me whimper. "Wait," he says, leaning back again. "If you don't want this, mate," he says. "Just say the word and I'll put a stop to it. I know times are..." His voice trails off, a deep groove forming between his brows.

"I want this," I say, kissing him again, quick and hard. "I need this. I need you, Tor. Please."

Lightning crackles in his eyes, the sight making a white-hot knot form in my core. Stars, he's gorgeous, all rippling muscles and surging power with a heart as big as his ego.

And he's mine.

All mine.

That is something to *cling* to, to revel in even when I feel like I'm drowning.

"Fuck, *Cari*," he groans, crushing his mouth against mine again. "We have time to make up for," he says, walking us toward my bed. "But it's going to be hard to take it slow with you."

He drops me on the bed, and I shake my head.

"Don't take it slow," I practically beg as I look up at him.

Tor smirks, the sight of the challenge in his eyes making every inch of my body tighten with anticipation. Slowly, he sheds his clothes, tipping his chin up with pure male pride as I linger over every inch of him.

Stars, I've not forgotten how massive he is—both in body and manhood—but *fuck*. Our separation these past weeks has only made this moment more intense, more needy, and I can think of *nothing* else but connecting with my mate.

He gives me the same heated, appraising look, and I swear I feel that intense gaze like a caress against my skin. I scoot back on the bed, widening my legs in a heady invitation. A muscle in his jaw ticks before he cocks a brow at me.

"Needy little wife," he says as he closes the distance, climbing atop the bed. He clutches my knees, pushing them apart even more as he quickly dips his head—

"Tor!" I gasp, falling all the way back as he licks through my heat.

"You taste just as good as I remember," he says against my flesh, spearing his tongue inside me.

I whimper at the intensity, my clit aching for pressure. I arch my hips, rocking against every lap, every thrust of his tongue as he devours me.

"Stars, Tor," I moan as he licks me slowly, torturously, as if he has all the time in the world to do just this.

"I've been dreaming about this sweet pussy," he says, glancing up at me, his crystal-blue eyes wholly animalistic. "Have you dreamed of my mouth, little wife?"

A warm shiver trembles over my body. The sight of my

massive warrior husband between my thighs is intoxicating. "Yes."

He smirks at that, reaching up to stroke one finger through my wetness. I jerk at the touch, my body so damn sensitive. He's holding me here on the edge, like pressing down on a piano key for too long before the chorus comes.

"And my cock?" he asks, his breath warm as it washes over my throbbing clit.

"Yes," I gasp the answer.

"I can feel you down our bond," he says, planting light, teasing kisses over my clit, my entrance. "You're so tightly wound." He wets his lips, eyes on mine. "Shall I make you unravel, little wife?"

"*Please*," I beg, not a shred of doubt or humility in my voice.

Tor smiles at my manners, then sucks my clit into his mouth so fast and so hard—

"Tor!" I moan his name as a flood of pleasure shakes my entire body, my orgasm ripping through me in a shuddering wave. Release barrels down my spine, and I fist the sheets as he licks me through the throes of it.

"Fuck, you're delicious," he says, shifting back, licking my flavor off his lips.

The sight has me shivering.

He moves across the bed, leaning back against the cushioned headboard before giving me a come-hither motion. "Come here."

I roll over, crawling between his massive legs, more than ready to ride him—

"Ah ah," he says, then twirls his finger. "Turn around."

Heat streaks through my veins as I do as I'm told.

Tor's powerful hands grip my thighs as he helps guide me backward until his hard cock glides through my slick heat, the motion like striking a match as he grazes my over-sensitive clit. He groans, rocking me back and forth a few times until my thighs tremble.

He bends his right knee, dragging mine up to match his, our left legs stretched out long as mine presses against his. The position situates his cock right at my entrance, my back against his chest—

He thrusts inside of me, and I whimper at the connection. Stars, he fills me in searing strokes that have my pulse skittering beneath my skin. I can't see him, can't know what he'll do next, and it only heightens the pleasure flooding my body.

"Stars, Tor," I groan, gripping his muscled thigh as he thrusts into me over and over again. "*Yes,*" I say when his free hand roams over my breasts, his fingers crackling with just a hint of the lightning that runs through his veins. The bite of pain has my nipples peaking beneath his touch, my breasts heavy and aching.

My head falls back against his shoulder as he drives into me, and he looks down at me, then down my body as he watches himself fuck me. It's overwhelmingly sexy, watching him watch us, and then he glides that hand down my stomach, the light electricity making every nerve in my body stand at attention.

"Look at you," he growls, pumping into me. "Look at how well you take my cock."

I cast my eyes downward, watching where he fucks me, watching as his hand makes it between my thighs—

"Tor," I groan, his crackling fingers tracing circles around my oversensitive flesh as he continues to thrust into me from behind. The sight is electrifying, or maybe that's just him, what he does to me. I go wholly liquid, my body flooding with searing hot pleasure that builds and builds with each stroke from Tor.

I close my eyes, surrendering to everything he's doing to me, using my body like it's always been his to play with. I'm nothing but pure sensation as he drives into me, as he rolls his fingers between my thighs, as he gives me just enough sting to push me right up to the edge.

"Sun, you're stunning," he groans, increasing his pace. "Fucking beautiful mate. Mine."

I tremble as his voice goes totally primal, excitement stealing through me at the way he shifts from teasing strokes to brutal, claiming ones.

"Tor," I say. "Tor I'm...I'm..." I can't get the words out. My breath is coming too fast as he pushes us both into a brilliant freefall that I never want to stop.

"Yes," he growls. "Let go, mate."

He slams into me, his cock sinking deep while he grinds his hand against my clit, and I cry out as my body shatters. I shudder as my orgasm comes and comes, sending tendrils of electric heat over every inch of my body. Tor follows me, and our release is so strong and sharp it takes me a minute to breathe, to see clearly as Tor slowly works us both down.

I lean heavily against him, limp and sated, my mind blissfully empty and my heart full. I arch my neck, managing to look up at him. He turns his head down toward mine, kissing me gently, lovingly.

"How was round one?" he asks, his voice a whisper between us.

I raise my brows at him. "Round one?"

I shiver again, my heart stuttering as he claims my mouth again.

Tor draws back, his effortless, cocky grin shaping his lips. "You didn't think we were done, did you?"

9

GESSI

"Thank you, your majesty," a female from the orchard village says.

I dip my head, handing her a parcel filled with information on the job she's been assigned while she stays in the Onyx City. It's heartwarming to hear her use my formal title, even when some of the Shattered Isle have labeled Cari and myself as false queens. It's even more endearing that most are happy to have positions and tasks offered to them to help them stay on their feet while being uprooted from their homes.

"My family is so grateful," she says, clutching the packet to her chest.

I swallow hard. "Huxton has been a starsend," I explain. "Without his generosity, none of this would be possible."

She nods. "We thank you both," she says, ushering her younglings who hid behind her away as she hurries out of line.

I blow out a breath before helping the next person awaiting assignment. There are hundreds who need placement, who need to work in order to maintain their rations and some semblance of normal life since they can't return home.

No one can.

Not until we win this war.

"I was told to come here," an elderly male says as he steps up to my table. River works at another one to my left, Huxton on the other side of him, and Crane is to my right.

"Were you given the special skills line number?" I ask.

He jerks a small piece of paper out of his pocket and shoves it toward me in answer.

I take the paper, quickly reading the list of skills. "You served in the previous Shattered Isle king's armies," I say aloud, and he grunts.

"Up until my retirement. And I didn't just serve, I led. I commanded over thirty-five hundred soldiers in my unit."

I raise my brows at his tone, but do my best to let it slide. Not everyone here is as grateful to be here as the previous female, and it's not hard to see why. They were forced to flee from their homes, choosing survival over submission when the general attacked.

"And you decided to stay loyal to my reign," I say, almost *ask*. Because many of the old soldiers sided with the general when he appointed himself a leader, and we're still on the lookout for anyone he planted within the survivors—like the male who attacked Lock. "Why?" I finally ask when he does nothing but puff out his chest.

"Because I never got along with General Payne," the male says. "I didn't agree with his methods. I still don't."

I hold my breath, feeling a *but* coming.

"But it's hard to pledge loyalty to someone who allowed their throne to be taken."

And there it is.

"When are you going to grow an ounce of courage and

take it back?" he snaps the question, and I set down his paperwork, folding my hands together as I look up at him from where I sit.

"When the casualties will be the least," I say. "Not that I owe you an answer."

"You damn well do owe me an answer," he grumbles, his tone rising enough that he draws Crane's attention on my right. He pushes away from his table, motioning for the male in front of him to wait. "You owe every single soul in here a stars-damned answer."

"Speak like that again to my queen and you won't live long enough to regret it." Crane's words are cold, lethal, and as true as his aim.

I'd be lying if I said the primal claim didn't *do* things to my body.

Everything Crane does lately has my body on high alert, wound tight with need since he's still so adamant he hasn't *earned* me yet.

But now is so not the time to delve into that whole situation.

"It's all right, Crane," I say, using my most diplomatic voice. "He's upset," I say, motioning to the male, who nods. "And I understand the reasoning behind it. I understand the confusion and the anger, but for now, you're just going to have to trust that we're doing everything we can to set things right in the Shattered Isle."

The male scoffs, and Crane leans over me from behind, one muscled forearm flexing as he presses his fist into the table, the position bringing him closer to the elderly male.

Stars, he smells incredible, that dark spice and rose scent surrounding me in a teasing caress that makes my heart skip. He's my mate, my stars-given mate, and we haven't completed the bonding process yet. Every day we go without completing it gets harder and harder—

"You don't intimidate me, youngling," the male says, looking at Crane like he's no more than a newborn. "I've been slitting throats since you were barely a thought in your mother's—"

"Benston, is it?" I cut over him, double-checking his first name.

He nods. "Retired general Benston Frant."

"I would like to put you in with those who are helping train Huxton's forces for the upcoming battle we have ahead of us," I say, and a sense of pride washes over his agitated eyes. "But if you want to stand here and argue with your queen and threaten her mate, then I have many other jobs I could enlist you for." I shrug. "We always need bait when setting a trap."

His lips pop open, but respect shapes his features as he nods. "Backbone," he says. "I like it." He bows at the waist. "Point me in the right direction, *my queen*. I'll whip the soldiers into shape."

"I have no doubts," I say, scribbling the necessary information over his paperwork before shoving it into a parcel and handing it to him.

He tries to take it, but I hold on to it a little longer, meeting his eyes. "Don't make me regret this," I say.

"I won't."

I release the parcel, and he dips his head to Crane before spinning around and heading out of the ballroom that has become our makeshift assignment center.

I sigh, but try to keep my smile light as the next person waits to be called up to the table.

Crane removes his fist from the table, and while drawing his arm back he lets his fingers just barely graze my bare shoulder. Warm chills erupt under his touch, that bond between us purring inside me, begging me to touch him back.

"We need to get Blaize back up here," Crane whispers in my ear, and the shock of that statement has me turning to look up at him.

And damn him, he looks so beyond good standing there in his leathers, his eyes sharp as he looks down at me.

"Why?" I ask, totally flabbergasted with the need slamming into me with him this close. He's more than made up for what happened in our past, but no matter how many times I tell him that, he still doesn't believe he's fully made amends.

"His skills are better served here," Crane explains. "He can tell when someone is lying." He nods to where the elderly man wandered off. "What if he is truly loyal to the old ways? What if he's here on the general's behalf?"

"I wondered that too, but he didn't feel like the other one did."

Crane cocks a brow at me. "Feel like?"

I shrug. "I don't know how to describe it," I explain. "The other male felt wrong. It was the way he looked at me, the way he spoke. Benston just seemed...angry. There are a lot of people who are angry, Crane. We can't assume every single one of them is here on the general's behalf."

He presses his lips together, a muscle flexing in his jaw. Stars, I want to feel those lips against mine. Right. Now.

I dare to reach up and gently touch his flexed forearm, the contact like a deep breath.

His eyes snap to the touch, then back to mine, reading the silent plea there.

"Soon," he promises, and draw my hand back. "Now, about Blaize—"

"Blaize's skills are better shared with the soldiers along-side Tor," I cut him off. "He can't sit here and listen to every single person. We won't become interrogators of these people, Crane. They've been through enough."

"Fine," he says, his tone rough. "But mark anyone you have suspicions of and we will have Blaize *feel* them out later."

"Fine," I fire right back. Stars, he's insufferable some-times. First with his avoidance of me and now with his total protectiveness over me without actually doing anything to protect my heart, which would be to relieve me of this emotional strain and complete the damn bond between us.

Crane goes back to his table, and I can breathe a little easier as the bond inside me settles in a weepy, whining sort of way. I motion for the next person in line to approach, and repeat the process I did with the two before.

It's hours before we complete today's assignments, and by the time I exit the near-empty ballroom, I feel half-dead on my feet. As much as my body is begging for a hot bath and a good long stretch of sleep, I head up the palace floors to Wynter's workshop, knocking before she calls me in.

She's certainly striking as she works at one of her long, stone lab tables, all manner of glass vials and burning beakers spread atop it. Her long red hair is braided back, showing off more of her smooth lavender skin, and red ribbons of energy tumble back and forth through the air, doing her bidding as she concentrates.

There are at least a dozen different flowers in small pots strung atop an adjacent table, and I immediately head that direction. I've been working with Wynter every night after I complete my queenly obligations, trying as hard as I can to create the All Cure from scratch. We thought that maybe me manipulating the genetic composition of other healing plants and combining them to create something new might offer a solution, but so far, all I've succeeded at is creating hybrid flowers that look pretty and have healing properties, but not enough to cure Lock.

"Are you sure you want to try again tonight?" Wynter asks without taking her eyes off her work. "Huxton says you were in the ballroom the entire day."

"I was," I answer. "And I'm sure."

She doesn't bother arguing, and I roll my neck as I center myself around my power. With the exhaustion, it's harder to coax to the surface, but I manage. Wynter and I work in a comfortable silence as we lose ourselves in our tasks, each of us trying our best to save Cari's mate.

She needs him on a level that's hard to explain to anyone who doesn't have a mate—like Wynter. I tried to tell her how vital a mate is after bonding, but she didn't really understand it. She totally understands the grief and sadness, but she believes life goes on, believes that Cari shouldn't succumb to this like she has...

But I know better. I know exactly how it feels to watch your mate almost die in front of you—thanks to the general's horrible power-draining poison he fired at us, but thankfully, it hadn't claimed my mate's lives. For a few seconds though? I knew what it was to lose them, and I never want to feel that way again.

"Damn it," I say, glaring at the flower weaving its way up to me, following the control of my power as a purple blossom unfurls before my eyes.

It looks nothing like the All Cure, but I can't throw it away yet. I have to run its properties against the poison and see if it will help.

"This one is potent," Wynter says after I pluck the bloom and hand it to her. "Incredibly potent," she continues, using her red ribbons of energy to squeeze the petals into a pulpy juice before looking at it under a microscope.

I hold my breath as I watch her work, using her power to draw one of the vials of Lock's blood toward her from where she has several stored. She mixes the purple flower's liquid with a few other solutions atop her workspace, then glances up at me before pouring it into the vial with Lock's blood.

We hold each other's gaze in silence for a few moments while she lets the two properties mix before putting it on a new slide and looking at it under the microscope again.

Her shoulders sink, and my stomach plummets.

"It's not a cure," she says, but there is hope in her tone. "But it is slowing the poison's cells down."

I raise my brows, life fluttering in my chest. "That's good, right? That buys us more time."

She steps away from her table, pointing toward mine. "Can you make more?"

I don't even answer. I whirl back to the table, looking at the steps I wrote down when creating this hybrid flower. My power groans, in desperate need of rest, but I jerk it to attention as I compel it to create more purple flowers.

"That's perfect," Wynter says after I've made six. "That's all we need for now."

She takes them, liquifies and mixes them before grabbing her black leather satchel and sprinting out the door, no doubt heading to Lock's quarters where he rests.

My muscles shake, threatening to give out on me until I cross the room and fall into a cushioned chair that rests in a small gathering of lush furniture in a back office in Wynter's lab. I think the witch lives here most nights, if the stack of blankets and pillows on a stone bench in the corner is any indication.

"You should eat this."

I jolt at the sound of Crane's voice, scanning the room until I spot him perched in a high archway of Wynter's office. He leaps down, landing softly on his feet, a bag outstretched toward me.

I take the offering, popping open the bag...

"Moon fruit?" I gasp at the sight of my favorite snack. "How did you find any here?" The dried fruit only grows in the orchard village and since the war started, trade production has been shut down for obvious reasons.

"One of the orchard residents gifted it to me after I helped evacuate the village," he says, sitting in the chair opposite me. "I saved it for you."

"Why?" I ask, taking a bite and moaning at the citrus flavor.

"It's your favorite."

I chew a little slower, my heart expanding in my chest. This isn't the first time Crane has done something like this since we've come to terms. In fact, he's gone out of his way time and time again to ensure I'm fed with my favorites, sleeping with the best, most luxurious blankets, or supplied with books when I need to escape the reality of our situation.

He's done everything and more to *earn* me, as he calls it.

"Thank you," I say before eating more of the delicious fruit. After I've eaten the entire bag's contents, I feel restored in so many ways.

"Were you watching me work out there?" I ask.

"I'm always watching you," he says. "You're incredible," he continues. "The way you create things, the way you breathe life into everything you touch..." He smiles. "It's beautiful, Gess."

I swallow around the emotion in my throat. "It's not enough."

He furrows his brow, folding his arms over his chest. "It's more than enough—"

"I haven't been able to recreate the All Cure," I cut him off. No matter how many times I've tried. I can *see* it in my mind, but I can't make it out of thin air.

"You can't create an ancient, rare flower that cures everything it touches?" he asks, eyes wide as he shakes his head. "Stars, Gess, what kind of earth power do you have?"

I laugh at his sarcasm, unable to stop. Crane joins in, and it breaks the tension that is always between us. It almost feels like it used to...before everything.

"I want to save him," I admit as our laughter slows. "I need to save him."

"You need to save your energy," he counters. "I'm all for healing Lock too. Trust me, I know what an asset that bastard is to this war, not to mention the idea of Cari losing a mate..." His voice trails off and he clears his throat as his eyes meet mine. "We have weeks, Gess," he says. "*Weeks* until all the armies will be ready and we can march on the general."

Fear and a good dose of hope swirls in my blood.

"You need to conserve your powers," he continues. "If you burn out, you'll be no match for what we'll face on the battlefield."

We'll face.

Because we will all be fighting. That's never been a question, but will we all survive?

"I know," I finally say. He's right. I know he's right. "But it's hard to conserve when all I want to do is help."

"We'll figure this out," he says. "I know we will. Cari will be okay."

He sounds so confident, but I'm not so sure. And with time running out...

"Weeks," I repeat him, eyes locking with his across the small table that sits between our two chairs. "Crane, what if we don't—"

"Don't do that," he says, standing up from his chair, heading toward the door.

I'm on my feet in seconds, anger replacing all the worry in my body. "Are you running away from me?"

"I'm not running," he snaps, whirling around as he reaches the door.

"Then why do you keep putting barriers between us?" I ask, stopping an arm's reach from him.

"Gess, I told you—"

"You have to earn me," I mock his tone, rolling my eyes. "Crane, we don't have time. Every day we're closer to this war. Every day I have to watch as my best friend's mate doesn't wake up. I have to watch her suffer and there isn't a thing I can do about it!" I blow out a breath. "But this?" I ask, motioning between us. "What we have. What we could have? It's right here. Right. Here. And you keep turning your back on it."

Tears line my eyes as the words catch up in my heart. Maybe he doesn't want this. Maybe all this *earning me* business has been an excuse to keep me close and protected but not connected.

"I'm not turning my back on it," he says, his tone sharp. "I'm not turning my back on you—"

"Then what is stopping you, Crane?" I snap. "What is it, really? And don't you dare say you need to earn me because you've more than earned my trust back—you've earned my heart, my *soul*."

His entire body is shaking as he holds the door handle, fight or flight evident as I finally have pushed him to his limit. But I can't find a fuck to give. We may have weeks left to live and I want to know what it's like to be with my mate, to feel our bond completed, to know that I've shown him every ounce of love I possess, to know that I've given myself to him in every way I know how.

"What is it—"

"I'm terrified!" he shouts over me, and I part my lips. "I'm terrified," he says much softer, his shoulders sinking.

"Of me?" I ask as he dips his head.

"Of what it'll do to you," he says. "If we complete the process and something happens to me. You've seen Cari. The idea of my death causing that..."

I gape at him. "So you think it's better to not be my mate at all?"

His eyes flash to mine. "No, of course not. You're all I want, Gess. *All*. *I*. *Want*." He shakes his head, his hand still perched on the door like he might fly away at any second. "But what if we do this, and I just hurt you even more? What if we do this, and I fail you again?"

My heart breaks at the pain laced in his tone, at the memories that haunt his eyes from what the general forced him to do. Forced him to watch as they tortured me because it was the only way he could save me.

"I won't survive it," he says, "if I fail you again."

I wet my lips, timidly taking the few steps between us until I lay my hand over his on the door handle. "You've never failed me, Crane. That's what I've been trying to tell you. You saved me in more ways than I ever knew about."

All those times the general made him watch, made him stand idly by, he suffered so I could survive. When he showed up when the general nearly killed me, when he saved us all. All the times since, with his attention to my needs, my moods...

"You've saved me every single day," I continue, raising

my free hand to his cheek. "I've loved you for longer than you know. And if we truly are going to face our deaths on the battlefield, I don't want to waste another *second* where you're not officially mine anymore."

Crane's eyes gutter, a shudder working through his body as his hand moves underneath mine.

I shut my eyes, my heart sinking as I feel him twist the door handle, likely to run away again...

The lock clicks, and my eyes fly open.

Crane steps toward me, cupping my hands in his cheeks as his eyes flash from my lips to my eyes and back again.

My heart is racing so hard I can barely breathe around it, this moment stretching into a thousand memories that have brought us to this exact spot in time.

"I love you," he breathes the words before pressing his lips against mine. The kiss is gentle and coaxing before he pulls away. "I've loved you more than I've ever loved anything in my life." He kisses me again, and I sigh between his lips, relishing the feel of his tongue against mine.

"More than your bow?" I ask, a smile shaping my lips as his eyes flare wide.

"Much more than my bow," he answers, walking me backward.

I've never seen him without the weapon, and I reach around, trailing my fingers over the line of it on his back. "How much more?"

He gently pushes me away, the backs of my knees hitting the couch on the opposite side of the chair I'd just sat in. I fall against it, unable to take my eyes off him as he removes his bow and arrows, setting them in the chair, followed by his shirt and the rest of his leathers.

I gasp at the sight of him bare before me, his smooth skin stretched over tons of corded muscle, black ink decorating his chest, his hips, and around his thighs. Stars, I've never seen anything as brutally beautiful.

"Let me show you how much more," he growls as he stalks toward me.

I don't wait for him to reach for my dress. I hop off the couch and slide the silk off, letting it pool at my feet before stepping out of it. The action pauses Crane in his tracks, his eyes flaring as he takes in every inch of me. He's seen me before, but right now, while we're alone, seconds away from taking our final leap together, it's like he's seeing me for the first time.

He doesn't balk at my scars, already knowing the location and source of each one. In this way, he knows me more intimately than even Varian, River, or Blaize do. And while we all work beautifully together as mates, this...this moment between us needs to be just us.

Crane moves so quickly I barely register it—one second, we're standing there, the moment tense between us, and the next my spine is kissing the couch and he's sliding his hands down my thighs.

"You're the most exquisite thing I've ever seen," he says, trailing kisses over my thighs, up my stomach, over my breasts.

I arch into the touch, lava streaking through my veins.

He works his way up to my mouth, slanting his over mine in a powerful, claiming kiss that I feel all the way in my toes. Stars, he can kiss. It's better than all the dreams I've had about it, all the fantasies I've conjured.

"Stars, Gess," he says against my mouth, his hands trailing everywhere he can touch. "Do you know how long I've waited to taste you?"

I go wholly liquid at his words, at the way he kisses his

way back down my body until he's hovering over right where I'm aching for him.

"Too long," he answers for me, because I can't remember how to speak.

And then he licks me, causing my back to bow off the couch. Fucking hell, his mouth fits perfectly against me, licking and lapping, thrusting and sucking. He's relentless, not stopping or slowing as I whimper, as I reach down and tangle my fingers in his hair, riding his tongue with sheer abandon.

"Fuck, Gess, *yes*," he says, the vibrations from his voice only adding to the pleasure roaring inside me.

He slides his hands underneath my ass, hefting me upward to eat me from a better angle, and I swear I see *stars*.

"Crane," I whimper his name, everything inside me a swirling buzz of need as he pushes me closer and closer to that sweet, sharp edge. "I'm—"

"I know," he says right before flattening his tongue against my throbbing clit, sending me spiraling in a hundred different directions.

I grip his hair hard enough to make him groan as I come against his mouth, my orgasm shivering along every edge of my body.

"Beautiful," he says, raising up on his knees before I've caught my breath. My head is still spinning from what he just did to me, but he hefts my hips high in the air until only half my back rests against the cushions.

In seconds, he lines himself up with my aching entrance and slams home, the angle letting him bottom out so deep I gasp.

"Fuck," he groans, pulling out to glide into me again.

And again.

The position renders me entirely helpless to his will. He

grips the globes of my ass, using it to yank me onto his cock in the most delicious way. I reach up and clutch the arm of the couch behind me, desperate to cling to anything while he absolutely owns my body.

His eyes are as sharp as ever as he looks down to where he thrusts, and he slows down, dragging his hard length out of me at a torturous pace. "Look how fucking perfect you are," he says, slowly inching his way back in.

It's searing and consuming and infuriating, the move coaxing all my nerves to life without plucking them for release.

"So. Fucking. Perfect." He thrusts to accentuate every word, and my body tightens around him until he groans. "Feels so fucking good," he growls, eyes coming back to lock with mine. "Do you like it like this, Gess?" he asks, going so slow I shiver. "Or does my mate want it harder?" he asks, going harder for a few seconds before slowing again.

My heart is racing, my head spinning so fast it's difficult to answer. Everything he does feels *right*.

"I want you slow," I say, clenching around him. "I want you hard. I want you fast. I want you whichever way you'll fuck me, Crane."

He goes totally still at my declaration for all of three seconds before he grins down at me, his grip on my ass tightening. "So fucking perfect," he says again, shaking his head before he unleashes himself on me.

"Crane!" My fingers bite into the arm of the couch as he pumps into me, each hard thrust bouncing off my swollen, needy clit in a tease that pushes me closer and closer to the edge.

He's fucking magnificent to watch, all those muscles tensing as he works my body, my mind, into a tight frenzy, and I can do nothing but hold on. He's in total control, and the bond between us is practically on fire as he slams into me again and again. It's like each time our bodies crash together, the bond between us grows stronger, glows brighter inside of us until it's impossible to think around. We're reduced to primal sensation and instinct as we give in to the bond that's begged for this for weeks.

Everything in my world narrows to where we connect, to the love radiating and swirling around that bond, and just when I think it can't get any more intense, Crane ups his pace, grinding his hips against me each time—

I shatter into a thousand pieces as release explodes across my body, Crane spilling into me as he pumps me through the waves cresting inside me. Our bond solidifies between us, shivering with delight at the completion.

I can feel him more than ever before, can feel the love and compassion, the protectiveness and the worry. It's all there and it's all Crane.

I fucking love it.

He gently lowers us to the couch, resting his head on my chest as we catch our breath.

My fourth and final mate has finally claimed his spot in my heart, and the piece of my soul that's been missing clicks together, making me feel whole in a way I never knew existed.

10

CARI

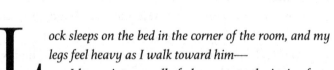

Lock sleeps on the bed in the corner of the room, and my legs feel heavy as I walk toward him—

I bump into a wall of glass, my teeth singing from the impact.

My palms fly up, feeling the glass, and I take a step back.

His cage...he's in his cage again?

Something climbs up my throat, tightening my airways. I knock on the glass, trying to get him to wake up so he can explain why he's in there again. Did Talon do this? Is this some sick joke?

Lock doesn't move.

I pound harder on the glass.

A hissing sound emanates from the other side, and I gasp as I see water spilling in from the corners of the ceiling.

"Lock!" I hit the glass over and over, screaming his name as I watch the water pour in. "Lock, wake up! Wake up!"

He doesn't move. It's like he can't hear me. How is he sleeping through the sound of the crashing water? It spills in huge waves that crash against the floor of his cage, spreading out and slamming up against the glass, but not seeping beneath it.

Stars, it's rising.

The water is rising so much that his furniture floats around the room.

And still, he doesn't move.

No. "Lock!" *I bring ice to my hands, encasing my fists as I throw all my strength into trying to break the glass.* "Please wake up! Wake up!"

Something bursts from the ceiling, and more water gushes in. It's so much now that his bed floats, and I watch, horrified as he slides off the mattress, his long, hunter green coat instantly soaking and pulling him under.

"Lock!" *I scream, hitting the glass over and over.*

It doesn't crack.

It doesn't shatter. Not even when I hit it with an ice hammer.

I turn around, tears streaming down my cheeks as my panic mounts. "Somebody! Please, help him! Help him!"

Silence.

I whirl back around, watching Lock as he floats beneath the now fully submerged room, watching as he doesn't flinch or jerk, doesn't wake up to try to find a way out.

"Lock!" *My voice is raw from screaming is name, my knuckles bleeding from hitting the glass so hard.*

I'm watching my mate drown and there isn't a thing I can do about it.

I keep hitting the glass, the surface impenetrable and smeared with frost and blood.

"Lock!"

His body starts to twitch as I watch his lips part, desperate for air that isn't there.

No, this can't be happening.

"Wake up!" *I scream, the muscles in my arms shredding as I pound and scream and—*

His body jerks violently before going completely still as he floats in the water.

My heart feels like it's being ripped from my body.

My legs give out and I fall to the floor, hands trembling and bleeding as I tuck my knees against my chest. I lower my head, sobbing so hard I can barely breathe—

"Why are you crying, darling?"

Chills erupt over my skin at the sound of Lock's voice, and I instantly snap my head up—

He's leaning over me, shirtless, his long black hair mussed from sleep. Our bed supports my back as I bolt upright, gasping for breath.

A nightmare.

It was a nightmare.

"Lock!" I cry out his name and throw my arms around his neck.

He wraps an arm around me, holding me to him. "It's okay, darling," he says. "It's was just a nightmare. I'm here."

For some reason, I can't stop crying, even as I cling to him, even as I feel his lips gently kiss my neck. I pull back, and he wipes away the tears.

His crystal-blue-green eyes are...sad as he looks down at me.

Why is he sad? Oh, no, he must've seen the nightmare too— we've shared so many dreams in the past because I've always left a spot open just for him in my mind. It's a sacred place, one connected by the bond that ties our fates together.

"I miss you," he says, his voice drenched in longing.

"I'm right here," I say, gently clutching his neck as I bring my lips to his.

He sighs at the contact, shifting backward as he draws me atop him. Stars, it feels like I haven't kissed him in so long—I'm desperate and hungry for it.

Lock's hands fly to my hips, holding me to him like he never wants to let me go.

"It was just a nightmare," I say between our kisses. "A nightmare."

But I'm still shaking, trembling from the sharp fear slowly building from the depths of my soul.

"Cari," he says my name like a plea, gently breaking our kiss to look at me. "I'm so sorry. I'm trying. I'm trying so hard."

I furrow my brow, trailing my fingers along his strong jaw. "What are your trying to do, Lock?"

A pit opens in my stomach the longer he holds my gaze.

I should know.

I should know what he's doing, what he's apologizing for.

I tilt my head, and Lock shifts beneath me, rising up so we're chest to chest, eye to eye.

His features pinch together, a groan of pain escaping his lips as if someone has stuck a knife in his back. He tenses beneath me, clenching against the invisible pain.

"Lock?" I gasp, scanning his body, running my fingers along every inch of him I can reach, searching for what's hurting him.

His groan turns into a feral growl, his hold on me loosening like his muscles are growing weaker. "I'm sorry," he breathes the words, and when he opens his eyes they look so heavy. "I can't stay any longer, darling."

Tears fill my eyes but I don't know why.

"What do you mean?"

"Always remember, you're my stars in an endless night sky," he says through heaved breaths. "Whatever happens..." He groans again, flinching like someone is carving him up from the inside out.

"Lock, please, you're scaring me—"

"Whatever happens," he says. "Know that. Remember that. I lov—"

He goes limp beneath me, falling back against the bed.

"Lock!" I lean over him, lightly tapping his face, trying to get him to wake up. "No, please. Please, Lock—"

I JOLT UPRIGHT, the breath in my lungs like razor blades as I try and catch it. Sweat coats my body, the ice in my blood thrashing like a threat is right on top of us.

I breathe in through my nose and out through my mouth, blinking the sleep from my eyes as I gain my bearings.

Lock sleeps next to me in his bed, unmoving save for his steady breath, still lost to the poison's hold. I'd left my chambers to come to his sometime late in the night, needing to be next to him.

It's been twelve days.

A nightmare.

A nightmare within a nightmare, only to wake up to one as well.

I rub my palms over my face, wiping away tears I shed in my sleep as I turn to face Lock.

Gessi and Wynter managed to create a tonic that has helped slow the poison's progression, giving him more time and bringing his vitals back to stable.

He's alive.

Lock is alive.

I repeat the mantra in my head every single time the nightmare bleeds into my mind. Every time I see Lock drowning right in front of me and not being able to do a damn thing to stop it.

I reach across the small distance between us, trailing my fingers along his jaw, down his neck until I rest my hand over the center of his chest.

His heart is beating. There is air in his lungs.

"Come back to me," I whisper, wishing I could fall back into the second part of the nightmare. At least there, I'd held him for a little while. "Please," I say, swallowing hard. "Please come back to me. I need you—"

"Cari," Talon's voice is a soft but concerned whisper from the doorway.

I roll over, sliding out of bed and crossing the room to meet him. "What's happened?" I ask, noting the severity shaping his features.

He glances behind me, sparing a second to look at his brother before returning his attention to me. "I intercepted another transmission from the palace."

My stomach sours, but I nod, hurrying out of my night-clothes and into a pair of silk pants and shirt, following him out of Lock's room and through the hallways of Huxton's palace.

Talon and I are the last to enter his workshop—Steel, Tor, Huxton, Gessi, Blaize, River, Crane, Varian, and Wynter already assembled around one of the larger tables to the left.

I don't bother sitting down, and instead nod to Talon, who brings up a recording on one of the monitors on the wall.

There are Shattered Isle people gathered in groups that form tight lines outside of the palace. The general is there, overseeing his guards as they distribute little bottles of some yellowish liquid I don't recognize.

"You all are smart in coming forward when I asked," he says, hands behind his back as he looks down at the groups from the steps of the palace. "Having powers is a privilege, not a right. This tonic will ensure they stay dormant until you've proven yourself worthy of them."

Gessi and I gasp at the same time.

The tonic. It's the same shit he injected Gessi and her mates with when he nearly killed them. It nullified their powers, made them weak and vulnerable in a way nothing else ever has, and now he's *forcing* anyone with abilities to take it? There are younglings in those groups!

I spot commotion in the third group, an elderly female who is refusing to take the tonic from the guard. The general heads that direction, a malicious grin on his lips as he stops before the female.

He says something I can't hear, something the recording doesn't pick up and the female—

She *spits* in his face before jerking down the cloth covering her shoulder, revealing a tattoo that...

Stars, it's the night-blooming flower I wear on my own arm. It's *my* tattoo—

The general swipes out in a motion so fast and so clean I barely blink before it's done.

The female's head flies from her shoulders, hitting another group member in the back before landing on the ground.

I stumble backward, and Talon's firm chest holds me up, his hands on my arms to steady me.

The general returns to the steps of the palace, looking directly at the drone he has recording him. "I've warned them," he says. "Whoever bears any marks aligning them to the traitorous queens will die." He wipes at his face, shaking his head as he turns to his guards. "The kingdoms were never meant to be ruled by the fickle minds and soft hearts of females." He glances at the groups, daring anyone else to show resistance.

They don't.

And the recording goes black against the wall.

That female died because she refused to submit. She

died because she bore my mark. She died because she believed in her freedom.

And her blood is on my hands, adding to the buckets that are already there.

"How far away are we from moving?" I ask, my voice lethally quiet.

"Three weeks," Tor answers.

"We still don't have official reports on the numbers the general holds," Steel adds.

"We're working on that," Blaize says. "We should have an idea soon."

Gessi shakes her head. "Three weeks? We can't move any sooner?"

"The soldiers aren't ready," Tor says. "We're making progress, but if we rush this, we may as well pick out their graves before we do."

I clench my eyes shut. More lives are in my hands—Gessi's and my hands. More people counting on us to keep them alive or let them die for a cause that frees others.

Exhaustion clings to my bones, sucking whatever life I have left right out of me. It's followed by a quick numbness that is both soothing and terrifying.

"Three weeks," I say. "I'm not waiting one minute longer."

Gessi nods, agreeing with me.

"I'll have them ready," Tor says. "I promise, little wife. I'll give you an army worthy of your rage."

I flash him an appreciative glance, then look to Wynter. "Any developments?"

She parts her lips, then shakes her head.

I nod, spin on my heels, and head out of the room.

I can't strategize any longer. Can't see any more recordings of the general slaughtering our people in cold blood. I can't...

Three weeks.

How in the stars am I going to make it three weeks without storming the palace to take back what's ours? To rip out the general's heart for what he's done to my mate?

I make it back to Lock's room, and slide back into bed next to him.

"I miss you," I whisper, tucking in close to his shoulder. "If you can come back to me, not only would it make me the happiest mate in the entire universe, it would also change the course of this war."

Lock's breathing doesn't change and his fingers are cool to the touch when I slide my hand in his.

"I need you," I say. "We all need you."

More than anyone likely even realizes. Lock is the most powerful being in the realms, without him...I worry how many of us will make it out of this alive.

11

BLAIZE

"How are they looking today?" Steel asks, coming to stand on my right side.

I stand on the balcony overlooking the training room, looking down at today's set of Onyx City soldiers. We had to split them into seven different units for training, and we've finally fallen into a rhythm of training regiments, shifting from my leadership to Tor's, Steel's, and back again.

"No one has fumbled their weapon today," I answer, arms folded over my chest. "So that's a bonus."

Steel lets out one of his lengthy sighs, the weight of it sinking my chest. We've been through battles together before, but what's coming...I understand why my friend is worried.

"They'll be ready," I assure him. "Huxton's training before we arrived has prepared them for defense. We're adding to their arsenal and adjusting their thought process to offense. They've improved eons since Tor got here."

Steel huffs a laugh. "Tor's inspiration and thirst for war is inspiring."

I laugh too, nodding. "He can definitely give one hell of a pep talk. I like yours better though," I add, bumping him with my elbow. His smile deepens, but it doesn't reach his eyes. Lock's lack of improvement has a whole hell of a lot to do with that.

"You really think they'll be ready?" Steel asks after we watch the soldiers below for a few moments.

"As ready as any soldier ever is for war."

"This one will be the most brutal yet," Steel says. "We've seen battles, sure. But nothing on this scale. This will change the course of our future. It'll rival that of the Great War."

The Great War. The mere mention of it has my hackles rising. King Augustus used me after the Great War to further enact his revenge after what King Jerrick had done to him.

I roll my neck in an attempt to stop the slow buzz building in my brain.

Necks snapping.

Bones crunching.

Blood spurting.

So many bodies. So many deaths.

My fingers tremble as the sound in my mind grows louder, as the memories swarm in from all sides. The All Plane king had forced me to do his bidding. He turned me into a living, breathing monster with no off switch. I've barely undone the damage he did, but I've gained a modicum of control since he died. Sometimes though, it sneaks up on me. Like the other night when the prisoner threatened Gessi.

"I never thought it would come to this," Steel says, shaking his head. "With the death of both my father and

Cari's, I thought we were on the brink of another wave of peace."

"There was never a wave of peace before," I say, instantly regretting it. Steel furrows his brow, and I shrug. "It may have looked like that on the outside, but on the inside?" I swallow around the clump of acid rising up my throat. "Your father ensured many were never allowed peace. Even after the Shattered Isle had been sequestered from the rest of the All Plane."

The buzzing sound switches to a sharp keen between my ears, and I clench my jaw.

Snap. Snap. Snap.

Thump. Thump. Thump.

"Kill them, or you know whose head will be next."

"I'm sorry that I never knew," Steel says. "I wish I could undo all he did—"

"Well, you can't," I snap, barely hearing myself over the ringing in my head.

Steel looks more concerned with my tone than hurt, and I flash him an apologetic look.

"I need...a break." The words are hard to squeeze past the tightness in my chest.

"Of course," Steel says, but I'm already bounding out the doors connected to the balcony, turning down hallway after hallway as I try to outrun this feeling.

Adrenaline spikes my blood, sending my pulse soaring as my head throbs.

Kill, kill, kill.

Kill so I can spare one life or another.

I turn down another hallway, the sound of King Augustus's voice raging in my skull—orders, demands, missions. Every time I returned, I came back with less of a soul.

My silver tattooed arm flexes, itching to wrap my fingers

around someone's throat and squeeze until I feel the satisfying crack give beneath my grip.

"It's what you're made for. It's what you're good at. The only thing you're good at. Killing." The king's voice is relentless, it's unending, it's—

Someone steps in my path and I don't think, I react.

One second, I'm alone in the hallway, the next my silver fingers are around a throat as I haul the person off their feet, slamming them into the wall and raising them high above my head.

The person kicks out, the pain barely registering in my gut as I pull him off the wall and slam him into it again—

"Blaize!" Gessi's voice, my *mate's* voice, cuts through the ringing in my head, silences the king's voice ordering me to kill, kill, kill.

The haze clears from my eyes and they widen when I see River in my grasp, gripping my wrist as he looks down at me confused.

I immediately let him go, stumbling backward until I feel Gessi's arms around me.

"No." I jerk out of her touch. "I'll hurt you," I say, shaking my head. "I don't want to hurt you."

"I'm fine," River says, gasping for breath. "I promise."

"Blaize," Gessi says as I bend at the waist, propping my hands on my thighs while I try to catch a breath. "It's okay," she says, rubbing her hands along my back. "Just breathe. *Breathe.*"

I shake my head, unable to do as she says.

She says something to River, and the two flank either side of me, maneuvering me into a nearby room before shutting the door.

I'm sitting in a cushioned armchair when my head finally, fully clears. When I can finally, fully breathe.

It's like a fog had slipped over my mind, my memories cloudy as I blink up and find Gessi and River sitting across from me with concerned gazes.

"Did I hurt you?" I ask Gessi first.

"Never," she says. "You'd never hurt me. Unless I asked you too," she teases, and the smirk she gives me sends heat soaring through my body, shaking away the rest of the fog.

I trail my eyes to River, but he waves me off before I can pose the question. "Honestly, I've always wondered what it would be like to be choked by that arm of yours," he says, and my eyes flare.

How can they both crack jokes? How can they both sit there, looking totally unafraid and at ease when I lost my shit out there? And for what? Because I can't control the memories?

"You should be beating my ass right now," I say to River. "Not making light of the situation."

River shrugs. "If you'd caught Varian out there like that, then I'm sure that would be the outcome. And if you want to lose to me in a fight, all you have to do is ask."

An involuntary laugh escapes me.

Gessi moves from her chair, crossing the distance between us, sliding behind my chair and leaning over it to run her hands over my chest. "What happened?"

I shrug. "Memories. Again."

She nods, rubbing my shoulders until I lean back in the chair, blowing out a deep breath. Each time her fingers dig into my tight muscles, I loosen another fraction. She's touching me, loving me, despite knowing I've been designed to kill.

I am more than what the king turned me into.

I am more than my ability to kill.

I'm a mate.

I'm Gessi's mate, and loving her is something I'm also very good at. Maybe even better at that than killing.

"I'm sorry," I say to River.

He waves me off again, his eyes wholly focused on Gessi and her massaging me.

The tension in the room immediately shifts as we all feel his thought process down the bonds that connect us. Fuck, it's intense. The longer we've all been together, the stronger it's grown. And now that Crane and Gess have finally completed the process, I can feel that bastard too. He's somewhere in the palace, likely training with Varian since I can tell he's close to him too.

Bonds are strange, but I wouldn't give mine up for anything. Not even if by giving it up it promised to erase all the memories of my past that haunt me.

Gessi's innocent touches turn a little more…intimate as she moves around to lean in front of me, working her way down my arms and back up, the motion causing her breasts to graze my chest and giving River the perfect view of her ass.

"Gessi," I say her name, my voice low and rough.

"Yes?" she asks innocently, as if she has no clue what she's doing to me, doing to *us*.

I shift in the chair, my cock hardening with each pass she makes.

"Do you know what you're doing to me?" I ask.

She smiles. "Loving you?"

I bark out a harsh laugh. "Sure," I say. "And making me crazy." I capture her chin between my fingers, gently holding her face close to mine. "You keep doing this to me right after I have an episode," I say. "It's dangerous."

She arches a brow, not moving an inch to break my

grasp. "You are dangerous, Blaize..." she grins. "To everyone else but me."

I shudder with her declaration, releasing her chin. Her face falls, her lips crushing against mine. I growl at the feel of her tongue against mine, closing my eyes against the worry pulsing in my chest.

Desire barrels down the bond between us, a flood of heat surging as she kisses me harder and deeper.

"Mate," I growl when she jerks her mouth away, her lips swollen from our kiss. Her eyes are lust-glazed as she stands again, looking down on me as River wraps his arms around her from behind.

"Needy, my queen?" he asks, taking the lobe of her ear between his teeth.

She gasps, nodding as she reaches up to wrap an arm around his neck from behind, turning her head enough so he can kiss her—

Fuck, I'll never get used to seeing this. Never get used to the ache that grows more intense inside me as another male makes her whimper. It's intoxicating and consuming.

River slides his hand beneath the front of her dress, raking his fingers over her breasts until she arches her ass against him.

"That dress is getting in the way," I say from where I still sit. "Take it off."

Gessi jolts at the demand in my voice, and I can barely hold back a smile as she does as she's told. My mate is so damn good at obeying, and it goes straight to my cock.

She shimmies out of her dress, kicking it and her shoes off to the side.

"Good girl," I say, letting every ounce of dominance leak into my voice. I know how slick it makes her. "Now, take off his clothes."

My mate trembles at the command before turning to face River, ensuring her luscious ass is on full display for me as she does it. Fucking tease. I love it.

River kisses and teases her while she works him out of his clothes, and I shift enough in my seat to do the same. My cock springs free the second I'm rid of my pants, a thankful sensation at being uncaged.

"Make her nipples hard," I demand, and River immediately spins her around to face me, playing with her breasts from behind. Her lips part on a breathy moan as River pinches her nipples before soothing the small hurt with light caresses, his lips trailing down her neck.

Fuck, she's so damn sexy, standing there on display while her other mate works her body into a tense frenzy.

Gessi reaches for me, a silent request in her eyes.

I smirk, rising from the chair, feeling like I'm standing up from a damn throne with the way she's looking at me.

"I bet you're slick," I say as I stalk toward the two of them. "I bet you're hot and wet for us both."

River groans as she rolls her hips, grazing her beautiful ass over his cock.

I look down on her, never breaking our gaze as I reach down with my silver tattooed fingers, dipping them between her thighs.

A hiss escapes my lips as I'm met with exactly what I imagined—she's drenched and needy.

I stroke through her heat, adding pressure only these fingers can manage. Gessi whimpers, riding my hand as I tease my fingers in and out of her.

River kisses her neck, her jawline, all while working her nipples into tight buds, while I tease and coax her right up to that edge I know she loves. She's breathless and tense, her entire body poised to pop off.

I draw my hand back, dipping my head to capture her whimper between my lips. She kisses me hard, her agitation at being denied clear in the way she bites at my bottom lip. I growl against the small sting, my cock dying to sink inside her.

She draws her head away, turning so she can kiss River. I watch with rapt attention.

"River," she says against his lips. "Blaize is edging me," she almost whines. "I'm *burning*. Please."

"I'll take care of you, my queen," he says, and I cock a brow at how easily he folds.

"Make her come and we'll revisit the chokehold I had you in a few minutes ago."

They both snap their eyes to me in shock, but there are equal levels of heat simmering there. I hold them both there in that moment, seeing if either will break.

They don't.

So I back up until I sit on the edge of the chair, widening my legs as I flick my fingers at her in a come hither motion.

She instantly obeys, but stops when she reaches me.

Fuck, that move alone makes me want to come. So damn obedient, waiting for instructions.

"Wrap those thighs around my hips," I demand, and she doesn't hesitate to straddle me, her slick pussy grazing right over my hard cock, making us bother shudder. I drag the tip of my cock through her heat, lifting her with one arm beneath her ass, dragging her wetness all the way down her slit and further.

She gasps as I graze that slickness over the seam of her ass, rocking against the touch.

"River," I say, motioning him over. "Work your way into this sweet ass."

I jerk her forward until my cock slides into her heat, her

walls hugging me in the sweetest fucking way. River situates himself behind her, doing exactly as I said.

Gessi moans as he works his way in, and it's seconds before I can feel him inside of her too. I take the reins, my hands on Gessi's hips as I lift her up and down, her pussy searing every time she sinks onto my cock, her ass no doubt tight and perfect as River drives into it.

I capture her lips, drinking in her moans as we find a rhythm, each of us working hard to make her as wet and dizzy with need as possible.

"Blaize," she groans when I lean back just enough that she rides me at a deeper angle.

River adjusts with me, his hands roaming over every inch of her body he can reach.

"*River*," she moans when his hand reaches around her to tease her clit.

She closes her eyes, her head falling back against his chest as she loses herself to the way we're fucking her. Her pussy flutters around my cock, and I reach up, wrapping my fingers around her throat.

Her eyes fly open, lust-charged as they meet mine.

"Come on my cock, mate," I demand, already feeling her right on the cusp. She grips my forearm, not to draw me away, but to hold me there, and that little move has me hardening inside her another degree.

I squeeze her throat a little tighter, just enough that her entire body trembles as she tightens around us.

"*Fuck*," I groan, everything narrowing to the feel of her pussy clenching around my cock, to the feel of River pounding into her from behind, all of it pushing me right over the edge with her.

Her nails bite into my arm, the sting making me come even harder inside her. She's liquid as River groans with his release, her moans joining ours as she continues to crash in waves of pure pleasure that show all over her face.

It's the most beautiful thing I've ever seen, watching her come undone.

I loosen my grip on her throat, slowly trailing my hand down her neck and chest. River kisses the top of her shoulder as we all catch our breath.

"You should try to kill me more often," River says. "If this is the result."

We all laugh, and I shake my head as we gently pull out of her, working to clean our mate up and get her dressed again.

"What room even is this?" River asks after he's dressed as well.

We all look around in confusion, not having a single clue where we're at, and that makes us all laugh.

"Poor Huxton," River says, shaking his head. "We've fucked in *so* many of his rooms."

Gessi's laughter is a melody that lifts my soul as she heads to where River is holding the door open for her. I finish situating my shirt, raking my fingers through my hair as I follow them out of the room.

For the briefest of moments, I forget that we're at war. I forget that the odds are stacked against us. I forget that I'm still struggling for total control.

I forget everything outside of the certainty that I have a mate who loves me beyond my faults, and three additional companions that have my back too.

It's a family I never thought I'd have.

And I'll do anything to keep them.

12

CARI

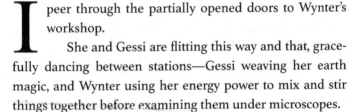

I peer through the partially opened doors to Wynter's workshop.

She and Gessi are flitting this way and that, gracefully dancing between stations—Gessi weaving her earth magic, and Wynter using her energy power to mix and stir things together before examining them under microscopes.

My heart expands in my chest but is instantly dashed by a heaping dose of...

Helplessness.

My friends are working themselves to the bone trying to create a cure for Lock, for my mate, and I'm doing...nothing.

I would give up all my power if I could have Gessi's abilities for one day so I could actually be useful. But as I am right now? Ice is no match for the poison keeping Lock asleep, keeping his powers weak.

My nightmare from the other night streaks through me.

"I can't stay any longer, darling." Lock's words echo in the back of my mind. The way he'd held me, the way he'd apologized, it was almost like he was *aware*.

But that can't be right, can it? His powers are flickers of

what they usually are thanks to the poison, I can feel that much down our bond. There is no way he had enough left to enter my mind and create that bridge between us...right?

Something calls to me, an answer just out of reach, and it leaves an unsettling feeling in my stomach. I look up again, watching Gessi weave her hands this way and that, creating yet another beautiful flower in hopes of finding a cure.

The uneasiness in my veins is more likely a testament to how miserably I'm failing my mate than any grand piece of a puzzle I'm missing, but I can't help it. It feels like that. Like I'm missing something just out of reach. If I could just wrap my fingers around it—

"You look like you could use a drink," Blaize says, materializing right next to me.

I jolt away from the door, breathing out a shaken breath at how quietly he snuck up on me. He flashes me an easy smile, then shrugs.

I spare one last glance at the pair working in the room, then swallow down another wave of guilt at being useless.

"Come on," Blaize says, motioning down the hall. "I found out where Huxton hides the good stuff."

I nod as I follow him down the hall. He's dressed in a casual pair of black pants and a shirt made of the same fabric, one sleeve torn off to show off his sliver arm. I've never really had the chance to study the array of tattoos. There's a little splash of red in the form of a star inked within the silver, and it really is as beautiful as Gessi has always described.

After weaving up and down hallways and climbing a few floors, Blaize finally holds a door open for me, ushering me into a simple little room that must be one of Huxton's studies. The walls are lined with ancient tomes, the floor lined with thick, decorative rugs with a few pieces of leather furniture that form a half circle around a stone hearth. There are two glass doors on the farthest wall that open up to a little balcony that overlooks Huxton's city below.

"It's beautiful," I say, stepping onto the balcony while Blaize remains inside, shifting books around on a shelf near an obsidian desk.

"Being the leader of a wealthy city has its perks, I guess," Blaize says as I turn back into the room, leaving the doors open to let the night in. It's a little crisp outside, but nothing that we'd need to start a fire for. And I can see the stars from an armchair facing the balcony. Stars that glitter in the night sky. Lock would love it up here.

My heart clenches, and I must show it on my face because Blaize cringes a little.

"Ah," he says as he reaches behind a stack of books. "Here it is. Another thing to add to the growing list of favors we owe Huxton."

He wags a crystal decanter before me, triumph in his eyes. Amber liquid sloshes back and forth as he heads toward me, not bothering to hunt for glasses. He takes a seat in the chair next to me, both the spots letting us look out onto the balcony at the stars.

Blaize takes a swig out of the decanter before passing it to me.

I take it, instantly taking a hefty swallow myself before handing it back to him. A sweet heat slides down my throat, sizzling with a delicious burn all the way down. I breathe deeper, letting the liquor kneed the tension in my chest.

"That is good," I say, leaning farther back in my chair.

Blaize nods. "Told you."

"And you found it...how?"

He shrugs, taking another drink. "Habit," he says.

I arch a brow at him. "You search for high-quality booze wherever you go?"

He smirks. "I scout every place I visit," he explains before raising the decanter and handing it to me. I take it. "Finding booze is just a bonus."

I take another drink, then hand it back to him. "Steel told me a little bit about what you do..." I say, then cringe. "I mean, what you were forced to do." Not that Steel knew his father was controlling Blaize at the time.

I sigh in disgust, seeing how even in death, our fathers are still haunting us from the decisions they made while alive.

"He told me about you too," Blaize says, his winter-blue eyes sincere as he hands me back the bottle. "Cheers to being forced to be assassins."

I huff out a dark laugh, and take another swig from the bottle. The drink is doing everything to loosen the tension clinging to my muscles, even going as far to chip away at the despair eating away at me. I welcome any oblivion self-medicating offers at the moment.

"One time," I say after passing the bottle back to him. "My father sent me to Sand's Swallow with orders to help oversee the village's harvest." I shake my head. "I didn't realize they were behind on the tax my father placed on them. He never told me things like that. He made it seem like he was ordering me there to help them but..." I swallow around the lump in my throat, gritty, soul-shifting remorse clinging to my insides. "After I check on the harvest, I received a transmission from him, stating there were criminals in the village that needed to be dealt with." Ice skates along my skin as the memories of those *criminals'* faces fill my mind. "Knowing what I now know about my father..." Tears prick my eyes but I blink them away. "I doubt they were criminals at all."

Blaize's features shift, a cool calculation slipping over his face like a mask as he nods in understanding. He takes another drink from the decanter, then hands it back to me. "An informer brought king Augustus a rumor of rebellion from the Air Realm," he says, scrunching his brow. "Had to be a decade ago." He shrugs. "He ordered me to dispose of the rebels at any cost. Went so far as to say they were sympathizers to the Shattered Isle." He doesn't look at me apologetically, and I appreciate that. We were at war. And even though we sought peace, here we are—different realms, same war. "He gave me the location and when I got there. They were young. Not younglings exactly, but young enough that they could've been taught. They probably could've been swayed. They were just caught up in something bigger than them." He sighs. "I tried to explain that, but the king didn't listen. He told me to do what I was conditioned to do and that if I didn't..."

His wintery eyes go distant, as if he's reliving the moment.

If he didn't obey the king, Steel would suffer. His best friend. The one person in his life he cared about before Gess came along.

"Kings can be the fucking worst." I take another drink, then hand it back to him.

"Fathers too," he says, and I nod. "Not all kings, though," he says after another drink. We've nearly drained the bottle. I don't even have it in me to feel guilty about drinking Huxton's secret stash. "Steel is a great king," Blaize continues.

"Yes," I say. "All of my mates are great kings." I think about them, about Steel and his compassion and heart, about Talon and his fierce protectiveness, his inventions that help his people, about Tor and his warrior's cunning and strength, his playfulness that keeps the spirit of the All Plane alive, and Lock...

My heart squeezes at the thought of him.

I look at the stars shining outside the balcony, thinking about that nightmare, about how real it felt. Lock should be up here with me, not Blaize.

Not that I mind his company, quite the opposite actually. As sad as I am that he's gone through experiences similar to mine, it's nice to have someone in my life that understands the mark they leave on a person. Being ordered to do what we did...being shaped and conditioned to be weapons instead of our own damn people...it's not something that everyone can comprehend.

I daresay I have a kindred spirit in Blaize, a friend for sure that I'm suddenly very grateful to have.

"You know if you ever hurt Gessi," I say, looking over him, "I'll encase you in a block of ice so thick even you won't be able to break out."

Blaize's grin is real and raw as he smiles at me. He leans a little over the armchair, drawing closer, his voice lowered. "And if you ever hurt Steel, I'll crush your windpipe like *that*." He snaps his silver fingers, and I laugh.

I actually fucking *laugh*.

I snatch the decanter from his hands, taking another fast drink. "Glad we're on the same page."

He grabs the bottle back. "I would do anything for Gess," he says. "She's a kindness I didn't deserve."

"I definitely never thought I deserved Steel," I admit. "He's too good to have been mated to someone with such a sordid history, but somehow he loves every piece of me."

"That's Steel," he says, sinking farther into his chair. "He sees the good in everyone. Sometimes to a fault." He eyes me, and I challenge him right back. "Not with you though," he hurries to continue. "I can tell how much you love him."

I breathe out slowly, suddenly missing my mates so much. They're here, but they've been working so hard on these war efforts, on protecting the people and places we can. And Lock, he's close but a million miles away. And I've been doing everything I can too, which is mainly keeping myself busy helping Huxton with the influx of people now residing within his lands. It's a good distraction, and I know it helps for the people to understand they have the support of their old princess, but it's hard to feel useful when I haven't changed the course of the war in any way.

Some inner instinct screams at me to return to Lock's bedside, to be with him even if I can't do anything about his condition.

"To living for our mates," Blaize says, taking another sip before handing me back the bottle.

"To dying for them too," I say, hurrying to take another sip as the words catch in my throat.

There is no denying it.

War is here.

There's no way all of us are going to make it out alive.

And if Lock doesn't?

Stars help anyone who stands in my path.

13

TALON

"**Y**ou're being a real asshole, you know that?" I lean my elbows on my knees, my brow pinched as I look at Lock. He's still lying in the same fucking spot he was when I checked on him yesterday.

I know Cari, Steel, and Tor are all taking turns moving him in his bed so he doesn't get sore, but sun damn me, it's like he's not even here anymore.

And I fucking hate it.

I shake my head, rubbing my palms against my face as I lean back in the chair I dragged next to his bed an hour ago. "You know, less than a year ago I was chasing you around the All Plane," I say, folding my arms over my chest. "I was *hunting* you, you little shit."

My throat constricts.

We thought he'd been slaughtering his way across the realms when in reality, he'd been killing assassins my father hired to kill *us*.

He'd saved us when we were hunting him down like a monster.

And now...

"You're too stubborn for this," I say. "Don't you remember the time the Corters breeched the palace walls?" I ask, giving him enough time to answer.

He doesn't.

"We'd barely mastered our powers, it was so long ago. They came in the night, ready to set fire to the walls." I blow out a breath. "Father ordered us all to stand down. He demanded we head to the protective barriers with his guards. He was terrified of losing us like he lost Mother." Acid crawls up my throat. When did those feelings change? When did he stop thinking of us as sons and started seeing us as threats?

"You didn't listen, though. You never listened."

Maybe he already could sense what my father tried to hide from all of us—a twisted hate that festered year after year.

Maybe he was just stubborn.

Maybe he just loved challenging our father any time he got the chance.

"You used your gifts and slipped us all past the guards," I continue. "You slaughtered a dozen of the Corters with your shadows. Shadows you barely knew what to do with. Even when you were outnumbered, you never surrendered. Even when you were exhausted, it didn't stop you from saving my ass when a Corter had a blade against my throat. You saved me." I rake my fingers through my hair, angry tears building in the back of my throat. "You saved me so many times. Even after I threw you in a damn cage."

Regret spiderwebs its way through my body, making my insides turn in on themselves.

"If I could build a machine that alters time," I say, staring down at my hands. "I'd go back. I'd do it all over. I'd save you. I'd tell you..." Something clogs my throat and it's hard to talk around it. "I'd tell you what a great brother you are."

I force myself to look up, to look at him.

His eyes are closed. His chest rises and falls at a steady rhythm.

"You didn't give up then," I say, standing up to look down at him. "Don't give up now. You hear me in there? Fight! Fight this—"

"What the hell are you doing?" Cari's voice cuts over my screaming.

Fuck, I was screaming at him.

She storms across the room, situating herself between me and Lock, the backs of her knees grazing the edge of the bed as she glares up at me.

"Do you really think screaming at him is going to wake him up?"

I fling my arms out, letting them fall heavily against my thighs. "It was worth a try."

"We're losing it," she whispers, and I can see the anger in her eyes, can see how it matches mine. I can practically feel our matched restlessness radiating down our bond.

"Yeah," I say, sighing.

"We could run, you know," she says, and I tilt my head at her. "We could pack a sky ship with enough weapons to sink an army," she explains. "I could sneak into the palace and slit the general's throat. I could end this."

Terror...*sheer* terror slices through my veins.

I grip her shoulders. "Don't you fucking dare say things like that."

Fire ignites in her dark eyes, and she jerks out of my touch. "Stop me," she says, crossing the room and marching out the doors.

I'm on her heels in seconds, reaching for her just as she

makes it around the corner near my rooms. I grab her arm, ducking into my room. I shove her back against the closed door, my chest heaving.

"*Don't*," I say again.

She tips her chin up, defiant. "We should," she snaps. "We should go. I hate it here. I hate being *useless* to everyone around me—"

"You're not useless," I cut over her.

"I can do nothing," she says, gasping against tears. "Nothing to help him." She throws her arm toward the direction of Lock's room. "But I could—"

"Stop," I say, no I fucking *beg*. "Cari, please. You can't do that to me again."

The memory of her sneaking away, leaving us behind to save Gessi from her father and the general's clutches steals through me, freezing my heart. I reach up, leaning my hands on either side of her face, caging her against the door. "I thought I lost you then," I say, leaning my forehead against hers. "I can't live through that again."

Our bodies are flush, and she trembles beneath me. "You may have to," she whispers.

I shift away enough to look down at her.

She shrugs. "This is war," she says like that is explanation enough. "Any one of us—"

I stop her words with a brutal kiss. She whimpers against the intensity of it, and I press harder into her before I jerk my lips away. "You will not die," I say, damning any of the fates across the realms to defy me. "You will not. I will not. We will survive." I slam my mouth against hers again, sliding my tongue between her lips until she fully opens for me.

Fuck, my mate tilts her head back in submission, letting

me devour her mouth in just the way I need to—hard and claiming.

She can't honestly be thinking about running away. If she was, she would've already done it. She's just blowing off steam, running her perfect mouth to me.

I drag my hand down her arm, intertwining our fingers as I pull away from her lips. "I did not wait my entire life to find you just to have you stripped away."

Cari's eyes are glistening as she looks up at me, her lips swollen from my kiss. I bring our intertwined hands up between us, resting them against the center of my chest. "You're mine. I told you that the second we accepted this bond." I send a burst of passion down it, and she shudders in response. "A war will not tear us apart."

"Just each other?" she asks, a tease in her tone.

I bark a laugh, and she joins in.

We wanted to tear each other apart when we first met, and not much has changed, except the love I have for my mate.

I release her hand, instantly filling mine with her ass as I haul her up and up until she locks her ankles behind my back. Her nose grazes mine as her arms fly around my neck.

"You want me to tear you apart, mate?" I ask.

The softest, most dangerous grin shapes her lips. "Always, Talon."

I nip at her bottom lip, and she wiggles against me. My blood is on fire with her declaration. I quickly scan my borrowed bedchambers, hating that I don't have my usual setup to properly edge my mate until she's a puddle for me, but I'm nothing if not adaptable.

I set her on her feet, stepping back to haul my shirt off with one hand. "Clothes off," I demand. "Then get on the bed."

She shivers at my commands, doing exactly as she's told. The submission goes straight to my cock, a steady heartbeat thrumming there.

Her ass is something to behold as she climbs on the bed, waiting on all fours for instructions. Fucking hell, my cock aches at the sight, at the patience in my mate.

"On your back, arms up," I say, and she flips over, crossing her wrists above her head.

I get rid of the rest of my clothes, but hold on to my shirt as I climb onto the bed. I kneel above her, reaching for her wrists as I secure them, the long sleeve shirt large enough to tie around them with the rest of the fabric draping over her eyes.

She gasps as I work, allowing me to bend and move her body in whatever way I want.

"Fuck," I growl at the sight of her. She's completely at my mercy. "You're such a submissive little mate," I say, gently gripping her chin as I lean over her, slanting my mouth over hers.

Cari whimpers at the unexpected touch. Taking away her ability to see or touch me with her hands only heightens the sensations stringing tight in her body. And I intend to pluck each and every one.

I suck her tongue into my mouth, kissing her hard and long and consuming. It's been too long since I've had her, and the separation is rattling all the way down in my bones. I need her like I need my next breath.

"Mate," I groan, kissing my way along her jaw, down her neck, until I reach her breasts. I kiss and suck her until her nipples are tight in my mouth. She shivers beneath my touch, her breaths ragged as she does her best to stay still. "You're behaving so well tonight," I say, unable to keep the smile from my voice as I trail a finger down the plane of her stomach, teasing her inner thighs. "I think you deserve a reward."

Her breathing hitches every time I slide my fingers near her sweet pussy, but she doesn't arch into the touch, doesn't break the rules by doing anything other than what she's told. My mate knows me, and I know what she likes too.

"What reward do you want, Cari?" I ask, kissing over her hips, the inside of her thigh.

"Your mouth," she breathes the answer. "Please, Talon."

"Fuck," I groan. "How can I resist those manners?" I dip my head lower between her thighs, flicking my tongue out in a little tease.

Cari moans, and I see her muscles tense as she keeps herself still.

I lick her again, her flavor coating my tongue and making my cock ache to sink inside her heat. She gasps, wiggling just a little before holding herself still. I grin against her, teasing her with light flicks and sweet laps until she's drenched and panting.

"You're so fucking beautiful," I growl against her. "And your *taste*...I've fucking missed your taste on my tongue."

Cari moans at my words. "Talon," she breathes. "Please, please..."

"Please what, mate?"

Her nipples are peaked, the sight of her all stretched out before me, with my shirt binding her wrists and draping over her eyes is the sexiest fucking thing. She's a tight string of need, all I have to do is cut her loose.

But she needs to say it first.

"Please make me come."

Fuck. Me. Those words coming from her mouth have me all kinds of tense, my entire body clenching, my cock begging me to pump into her wetness.

I hold my ground though, wanting to stretch this moment into a thousand.

I'm silent except for my harsh breaths, which brush over her heat in warm bursts. Her breathing is still ragged as she waits for my response or waits for a command. I hold her there in anticipation before slipping my hands underneath the globes of her ass and hefting her off the bed a little.

Then I unleash myself on her.

I plunge my tongue into her glistening pussy, spearing it in and out, relishing each time she shakes against my face, each moan that slips past her lips.

"Talon," she moans, her arms still above her head, her ass in my hands and my face buried in her pussy.

I rock my head up and down, using my bottom lips to drag along her swollen clit. It's not enough pressure for her and I know it. I don't want her coming just yet. I want to walk her right up to that edge and hold her there until she can't breathe around the need.

Because that's where I'm at. I'm living in that sensation, living in the brutal, beautiful place between anticipation and release and it's the fucking best with her.

"Stars," she gasps. "*Talon.*"

"Want me to tear you apart now?" I ask against her slick flesh.

"Yes!" she says. "Tear me apart. Fuck me however you want. Just do *something.*"

I grin against her before dragging my teeth over her swollen clit, sucking it hard and fast—

"Talon!" She cries my name as she falls apart around my face, her thighs clenching my head as she shakes with her orgasm. Her flavor bursts on my tongue, and I lick her through the cresting waves, using the leverage on her ass to rock her up and down until she's gasping and shivering.

After a few moments, I lower her back to the bed, licking my lips as I drag my hands along her body, rubbing and grazing every inch of her until she's all wound up again. Her body is sensitive from the orgasm and she's so fucking responsive to my touch, gasping or arching into it, the rules all but forgotten.

And I don't care.

Right now, I don't care about the game.

I just want to fuck my mate.

And I want to see her eyes while I do it.

I work my way up her body, kissing and nipping her sensitive flesh before I pull the shirt away from her eyes, and release her from her bonds. Her arms immediately fly around my neck, and I haul her upward, until her thighs are hugging my hips.

I'm on my knees, holding her up and flush against me, and she's all slick heat as she rocks herself over my aching cock. I palm her ass, holding her gaze as I situate her above my cock, nudging her entrance.

She clings to me, her breasts grazing my chest as our breaths match in speed. I keep holding us there, scanning the lines of her face, her lips, and back to her eyes.

I've missed her so fucking much it hurts.

Pure, undiluted need and love spiral down the bond, jolting me with the intensity of it. How can she love me as much as she does? Especially with how we started as volatile enemies? How did I get lucky enough to deserve a mate like her?

She inches forward, grazing her lips over mine, teasing her tongue into my mouth as she takes control of the kiss. I groan against the taste of her, and let her ass go.

"Talon!" She gasps as she sinks atop my cock, taking me to the hilt in one move.

I shudder at the feel of her. She's slick and hot and hugs my cock in all the right ways. Fuck, I'm home. I'm fucking *home*.

I rise off the bed a little, pumping into her before sinking back down. She keeps kissing me, moaning into my mouth with each thrust I make. I increase my pace, gripping her ass again as I take full control, fucking her from beneath. Her breasts grind against my chest as she keeps us flush, her tongue rubbing against mine before she sucks it into her mouth.

I groan, heat spiraling straight to my cock. I jerk into her, pumping harder, faster, wanting to absolutely consume her.

"Yes," she sighs between my lips. "Stars, yes."

She throws her head back, gasping for breath as I pound into her, grinding against her clit with every thrust. Her eyes are lust-glazed and heady as she looks at me, her lips swollen and parted on her ragged breaths.

She's the most beautiful thing I've ever seen, and she's mine. All fucking mine.

I free one hand, reaching up to tangle my fingers in her hair, arching her head back so I can have full access to her neck. I kiss the soft patch near her collarbone before I bite it, and she jerks against me, moaning as she gets even more slick around my cock.

Fuck, if she keeps doing that—

"Again," she demands, her nails digging into my shoulders. "Mark me again, Talon."

Liquid fire soars through my body at her demand, and I fly to the other side of her neck, biting her there.

She rocks against me again, hard and fierce as I pump into her.

"More," she begs.

I keep my hand in her hair, gripping it tight as I work my way down, biting the top of her breast—

"Stars!" she cries out, her pussy clenching my cock like a hot vise.

Fucking hell, my mate. She's perfection. She's absolutely fucking *made* for me.

"Again," she says, breathless. Her nails are biting so hard into my skin I know she's marking me too. She's wild and relentless, rocking into me in rhythm to my hard thrusts. "Talon, please. I'm there. I'm right—"

I bite at her other breast, sucking her soft skin hard enough to mark her.

Her pussy flutters around my cock, and my name is on her tongue as she shakes around me. Her orgasm pulls on me, shattering any resolve I had to hold out. Lightning streaks through my veins as I come inside her, spilling over and over again with brutal thrusts that have her fluttering yet again.

She's liquid as she takes all of me. I can feel her desire my thighs and I fucking love it, relish that she's unraveled so much for me.

We're both trembling as we come down, our foreheads pressed together as we breathe through the intensity. After a few moments, I gently pull out of her, hurrying to clean us both up before tucking her against my side under the covers.

Her breathing grows long and even, her eyes heavy as she looks up at me, lazily tracing the lines of my goatee. "I love you," she whispers, her eyes fully shutting.

Her hand falls heavy against my chest, and I cover it with my own, holding her against my heart.

"In this life and the next," I whisper.

14

CARI

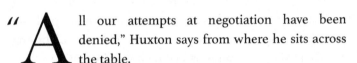

"All our attempts at negotiation have been denied," Huxton says from where he sits across the table.

We're all gathered in Talon's workroom again, Steel on my left, Tor on the other side of him, and Talon on my right. Gessi and her mates fill out the other half of the table, and Wynter sits on Huxton's right.

It's been another week and Lock still sleeps. Any hope I had that he'd wake up and ride off to battle with me has completely disappeared.

"Of course," Gessi says. "We anticipated that."

Huxton nods, his golden eyes warry. "Where are we with the soldiers' development?"

Tor clears his throat, sliding his palm across the table. "They're ready. Another week, and they'll be a force to be reckoned with."

A *week*.

That's all I have to wait until I can drag one of my blades across the general's neck. Adrenaline and anticipation storm through my blood, the ice in my veins crackling with need. I will end him in every way imaginable for what he's taken from me.

"Have you made any progress, Wynter?" Steel asks, his voice soft.

Wynter shakes her head, disappointment in her eyes. There are bags under them too, and a stab of guilt hits me in the chest. She and Gessi have been working themselves to the bone trying to help Lock.

"We do have something," Wynter says, and my heart lifts. She nods to Gessi. "We were able to concoct an antidote for the poison the general used on Gessi and her mates the last time they met."

My chest deflates even when I know I should be thrilled.

"You found a way to counteract the loss of our powers?" Talon asks.

"Yes," Wynter says. "Well, not counteract, but prevent. It only works in small doses, so we've condensed it to capsule form. You'll have to take them into battle with you. I've already had the tailor work on each of your fighting leathers to install a holder near your left shoulder."

Irrational irritation snakes through me, making my muscles tight. I can't help but cut my eyes to Gessi, wondering how long the two of them spent on this cure and not the other? It's wrong, I know it, I can feel it in the bitter taste it leaves on my tongue, but I can't stop it. Who knows how many hours they dedicated to this vital tool for the upcoming war. Hours that could've been spent trying to save Lock.

Gessi flashes me an apologetic look as if she can read my mind.

I jerk my eyes away from her, shame unfurling beneath my skin. I can't be angry with them. I can't be. Having something that prevents the loss of our powers is a *huge* advantage for us, but I can't help wishing finding a cure for Lock was just as easy.

"Thank you," Steel says, glancing at Wynter and Gessi. "I know that couldn't have been easy."

"It wasn't," Gessi admits. "Between the two of us, we're practically stripped raw from trying so many different cure combinations."

Wynter's shoulders drop. "We're still trying for the All Cure."

I swallow around an angry lump in my throat, my heart shattering at the realization that if they keep going at the pace they are, they won't last a second in battle. They'll die. And that will be on me. Because of my need to save Lock. I'll lose my sister because of sheer selfishness.

"You should stop," I say, and all three of my mates snap their eyes to me. Their looks of shock only make my heart break a little more.

"No," Gessi says. "There is still time. We didn't think Lock would survive the first week, but he did. He's defied all the timelines we've given him. There is still a chance—"

"There's no chance," I cut her off, tears climbing up my throat. I focus on my raw anger to turn them to ash. "No chance. None. You two are burning out. And we need you strong for what's coming." I blow out a breath, my heart shattering. "Let's put an end to it. Conserve your energy—"

"We can keep working," Wynter argues. "We're—"

"Burning. Out." I practically growl the words. "Wynter, I've seen your incredible power. I need you to rest up and conserve it. I need you at your full strength to help protect Lock in case the general sends a team to finish what he started." I shake my head. "I can't march off to battle without knowing he's protected."

She straightens her spine, looking very much like she

wants to argue with me but can't deny my logic. She gives me a nod. "I'll keep him safe."

"We will," Huxton adds. "With everything that we can. I promise you."

I dip my head in appreciation. There is relief in knowing they'll defend him, but I can feel myself hollowing out by the second. I feel like I'm failing him all over again by telling them to stop searching for the cure, but I can't risk their lives for the sake of my mate. Even if I selfishly want to.

"I'm not going to give up on your mate," Gessi says, and I tilt my head at her. Can't she see that hope is slowly killing me from the inside out? Every day that Lock doesn't wake up...Stars, it's like a piece of me is dying right alongside him. "I'm not," she says, defiant at my silent plea. "We have a week. I'll rest like you said, but Varian and I have been talking," she says, eying her mate. He nods at her encouragingly. "We have little doubts the general took the All Cure from the Stone Realm. I intend to find where he stashed it. If I can just see it, touch it, I'll be able to recreate it."

And if Lock can just hold on until then—and if we can all survive—then we'll all live happily ever after.

I don't believe it.

I can't even see the bright future she's trying to manage.

I *can't*. I'm too numb, too raw, too everything.

"How to you propose to find it in the middle of a battle?" Tor asks, not chastising but genuinely intrigued.

"Cari and I are going to use the secret passages we built when we were younglings."

I raise my brows at her, but it's Talon who huffs. "We exposed those tunnels when Cari breeched them to save you."

Gessi's eyes meet mine, and a flicker of hope spears

through me. Damn it, I need to stop that. It's going to kill me in the end.

"Not all of them were exposed," I say, and Talon gapes at me. I shrug. "We made dozens together," I explain. Secret tunnels from the palace made from ice and earth by two best friends who were desperate to escape their cages.

"There is no way the general knows about them all," Gessi says. "Cari and I will use them while you all draw him and his armies out."

"You want us to provoke him into a battle?" Tor asks.

Steel shakes his head. "He won't be prodded like that," he says. "He'll keep himself protected in the stronghold of the palace and just send his armies to fight us."

"We need something to draw him out," Talon says.

"An offering," Blaize adds, arms folded over his chest. He looks at Gessi, then me. "What does he want most?"

Gessi blows out a breath, contemplating as she looks to me. Varian and Crane do the same, the four of us bonded by our equal trauma delivered by the general. I bounce from friend to friend, our conversation silent as we deliberate.

And then it clicks, hitting us all at the same time from our shared looks of realization. Varian gives me a nod, and I wet my lips.

"We offer a trade," I say.

"For what?" Huxton asks.

"We offer him rule over realms in the All Plane in exchange for peace."

"What?" Talon snaps.

"He already has some of his armies occupying the Stone Realm and smaller territories across the Shattered Isle. You want to give him more?" Steel asks.

Tor laughs slowly, nodding as pride gleams in his eyes. "Clever little wife."

"Think about it," I say. "He'll come in person to hear the offer."

"He'll bring the entirety of his army with him," Tor says. "Thinking it will be enough to protect him if we break peace and attack."

"Which we will," I add.

Talon and Steel share a look, and I can see the distaste in Steel's blue eyes. My honorable mate, my wholly *good* mate, down to his core.

"I know it's not honorable," I say. "But the general doesn't live by any code. He's murdered and tortured and taken from all of us. There are no cordial years-long wars with him. We have to rip him out by the roots." Just like he did any chance at saving Lock. "We have to play as dirty as he does in order to stop him."

Blaize meets Steel's gaze. "She's right, Steel," he says, and my heart warms toward him all over again. A true friend, he's got my back even in the grimiest of situations.

"I know she is," Steel finally says. "I know what we have to do."

Relief uncoils inside me at having the support of my mates, my friends.

"We'll need to send some smaller, elite units to the territories the general is occupying," Steel adds. "If we're doing it this way, we need to hit him in every possible direction. End it all in one clean swoop."

"We'll start work on assigning teams tonight," Huxton says, eying Tor across the table, who nods.

"We have a plan," Steel says, pushing away from the table. "Let's get to it."

Everyone stands, lingering as we break into groups and talk in hushed conversations. Crane glides his fingers along Gessi's jaw, beckoning her out of the room before I have a chance to speak to her. Warmth radiates in my chest at the sight, happiness gliding through me that the two have finally worked everything out.

It's a good thing, to have the bonds completed before we march against the general. It'll make her stronger, more fortified in what is to come.

Tor and Blaize and Steel follow Huxton out of the room, heading to create the elite teams while Talon works on contacting Storm in the All Plane to fill him in. Wynter trails after Huxton and the others, Varian and River flashing me comforting looks before heading the same direction Crane and Gessi went.

Everyone has their priorities right now.

Everyone but me. Because I'm not a healer or a warrior trainer or a war strategist who needs to give reports.

I'm a weapon.

I always have been.

And I can't be utilized until we're on the battlefield.

LOCK SLEEPS SOUNDLY next to me as I sit on his bed, a sleep tonic in my hands. It's the day before we march on the palace and sleep is the farthest thing from my grasp but my body and powers desperately need it.

The general has agreed to meet us to discuss which realms in the All Plane he wants possession of, just like we anticipated. All we have to do now is pull off the rest of the plan. And for us to be able to do that, I really need to rest.

But I can't stop thinking about that *something* that has been bothering me since my nightmare about Lock. Like there's an answer within reach, I just have to look in the right direction.

I bring the tonic to my lips and swallow it down, discarding the vial on the nightstand next to the bed as I lay on my back, lacing my fingers through Lock's hand. He doesn't stir, doesn't respond to my touch, and I hate that I've grown used to it. Hate that I've come to expect his stillness.

He's *never* still. From the moment we first met—the moment he tried to capture me in the Air Realm, his blade to my throat—he's never been this still.

Sleep hangs heavy over my eyes, the tonic working its way through my blood. My limbs loosen, my breaths deepening as I close my eyes.

I think about his blade against my throat, fondly thinking at how many times he's held it there.

When he was in his cage and we had our secret meetings...the first time I let him in my mind, he held a blade to my throat. Held it there but never broke my skin, held it there but—

Sleep swarms over me, coaxing me back and back into my own mind, but I cling to that memory. Letting it play out. Going over every detail.

My heart jolts despite the rest of my body being so heavy.

I'd taken control of his illusion that night.

I'd been able to manipulate it as if I were the one spinning it.

It had shaken Lock because it'd never happened before, and I remember thinking it was simply because of our bond.

I spin in the darkness, my mental awareness rippling between sleeping and waking thanks to the tonic.

We've shared dreams before, and I always thought it was because I kept that spot open in my mind for Lock, but what if it's more? What if our bond creates a mental connection thanks to his power that can be used both ways?

What if the nightmare I had...what if Lock had really been there with me?

What if—

My palms press against the glass cage, cool to the touch.

Lock is on his bed, sleeping, unmoving, and the water...fuck, the water is already pouring in.

Not again. No, please. Not again.

I can't watch him drown again.

Damn the sleep tonic, I should've stayed awake. I'd rather be tired on the battlefield than watch this again.

But I can't tear my eyes away.

Can't stop from pounding on the glass.

The nightmare is potent, despite me knowing what happens.

The water crashes in, rising and rising—

"You came back," Lock's voice radiates through my entire being.

I turn my head to the right, looking up and up at him as he stands stoically next to me, his arms folded behind his back as he watches the water fill the cage.

"I'll always come back for you," I say, turning to face him.

He points to the cage. "I've watched this a thousand times," he says, his voice way too calm. "I've tried a million different ways to change it, and it's always the same."

My heart races in my chest as I look at the scene. The water has made its way to the bottom of his bed. The chairs are already floating, the table where he keeps his books upturned.

I tear my eyes from the scene, reaching out and gripping Lock's hand.

"Is this real?" I ask, and he turns toward me. His eyes are more green than blue right now, and they're filled with longing, regret, anger. "Or am I just dreaming again?"

Lock's hands cup my face as he leans down, gently slanting his lips over mine.

I sigh at the contact, fisting his shirt to draw him closer. Our bodies are flush and he shifts us until my back is against the glass, the sound of rushing water crashing around us.

He deepens the kiss, his tongue rubbing against mine as he sweeps in, devouring my mouth and stealing my breath.

Heat swarms my body, tingles shooting all the way to my toes. Stars, his kiss. It's chaos and mischief, smoke and shadows.

It's always been my undoing as much as it's been my salvation.

"Lock," *I whisper his name between our lips, my pulse fluttering with every graze of his mouth against mine.*

He pulls back, our chests heaving from the kiss, and he looks down at me. "Does that feel real, darling?"

A warm shiver makes my body tremble as he runs his thumb over my bottom lip. I nod, breathless.

"Then that's real enough for me." *He swoops down again, claiming my mouth with a carnal bite to it. Stars, I never want to leave this moment. I never want to stop feeling him—*

Another crash of water shakes us out of the kiss, and I turn to look at the water filling the cage. It's close to overtaking him again.

Panic spears down my spine.

"Every time," *he says, disappointed. He slams a fist against the glass, enough to make it shudder but not break.* "I can't change it."

My mind is whirling, panic constricting my throat as that water keeps crashing in. I snap my head up to his. "Maybe we can," *I say, reaching for his hand again, lacing our fingers once more.* "Together."

He tilts his head, eying me skeptically. "But if this is just a dream..."

I place my free hand on the glass, ice spiderwebbing its way across the surface. "Does that feel real?" *I ask.*

He moves his free hand over my ice, hissing slightly. "Yes."

"Then that's real enough for me," I echo his words.

Silently, we count to three, his hand clutching mine in a fierce grip while we slam all of our collective power against the glass.

Ice and shadows swirl together, combining to create something entirely new, something glowing with power and radiating strength unlike anything I've ever felt before.

Our minds meld, that pathway between us open and surging as we hit the glass with that new power over and over again.

The water reaches the top, Lock's body already floating through the abyss.

No.

No, I won't fail.

We won't fail.

Not tonight. Not now—

The power between us surges, our bond searing with a white-hot heat that threatens to burn us both to ash.

But I keep pushing.

He keeps pushing—

The grass cracks. Snaps. Shatters.

And the force of the rushing water throws us off our feet, disconnecting our hands as we slam into the wall behind us.

"Cari!" Lock yells for me, reaching for me as we're shoved in opposite directions, the water acting like it has a mind of its own as it moves.

"Lock!" I reach back for him, my arms flailing as the water takes me under, rushing me down a dark hallway, farther and farther away from him.

"Cari!" His shouts are garbled, water threatening to choke him. "Cari!"

. . .

"CARI," Steel's voice is soft and I can feel the warmth of his hand on my cheek.

My eyes flutter open, panic stealing through me as I gasp for breath. I shoot up in bed, expecting to be soaked with the water that almost drowned us—

Us.

I whip my head to the right, and a breath rushes out of me.

Lock is sleeping.

Lock is *still*.

I rake my hands over my face, forcing life into my limbs.

"It's time, mate," Steel says, his warm hands grazing over my shoulders. "We have to go."

The battle.

The plan.

The death of the general.

Nothing less could tear me from Lock's bed.

Nothing less could stop me from trying to dream again, trying to reach Lock again.

I nod, swinging my legs over the bed, and standing to wrap my arms around Steel. He holds me to his powerful chest, stroking his fingers through my hair.

"Did you have another nightmare?" he asks as if we have all the time in the world to discuss it.

I swallow hard, the images of the water crashing out of that cage washing over me. My lips tingle like they can still feel the effects of Lock's kiss.

"Just a dream," I say, sighing against him. I turn, looking up at him.

His blue eyes are sincere and loving with a heaping dose of concern as he looks down at me. "Are you ready for this?"

I look back at Lock one more time, swearing I see his fingers twitch. I hold my breath, but I must've imagined it because he doesn't move beyond his soft breathing. I turn back to Steel.

"What if I'm not?" I whisper, the sensation of stepping off a cliff yawns awake before me. I'm terrified to take one step out of this room, because if I do...I may never come back. I may never make it back to Lock.

Steel bends down, pressing his lips against mine.

It's amazing how different each of my mate's kisses are.

Lock's is chaos and mischief.

Tor's is all electricity and fun.

Talon's is severe and brutal, but Steel's? His is pure warmth and passion, love and understanding. His kiss fills me with a solid, renewed energy that brings me nothing but hope.

He guides me to my room, helping me into my fighting leathers, silent but supportive as he zips me up, his touches lingering in some areas longer than others. When he's finished, I match him in leather and thin armor. No doubt the rest of my mates are wearing the same thing.

Love radiates down our bond, and I cling to him one last time, kissing him as memories storm me.

Steel was the first of my mates to accept me, to *love* me, to care for me. It started with his kindness, and now, as we prepare for the biggest battle of our lives, I'm comforted knowing it's him guiding me out of Huxton's palace and onto a sky ship.

It started with Steel, and as we fly toward the palace, I keep hold of his hand, squeezing it and praying to the stars above that the rest of my mates make it out of this battle alive. Because leaving Lock behind feels final in a way that makes a piece of me die inside, and I know I won't survive losing anyone else.

Talon slows his ship as we approach the royal city's borders. We don't have time for a full stop, and despite having held Cari's hand throughout the entire trip here, I still don't want to let her go.

There is a pit in my stomach, opening wider the closer we get. I've been in dozens of battles before. I've been outnumbered before. But I've never been as afraid as I am now.

Because I have something to lose.

Cari.

With Lock's condition, grief already sloshes in my blood, but having to let Cari go? It's one of the hardest things I've ever done. I know she and Gessi are incredibly powerful and more than capable of handling themselves, but this...this is war.

I watch as Cari kisses Talon goodbye—it's a harsh, claiming kiss that bends them both. She already said her goodbyes to Tor before we left earlier, and Blaize is doing much the same with Gessi right now.

Fuck, Cari is heading toward me now, looking like a

goddess of death and ice in her obsidian fighting leathers, a corset of armor cinched tight around her torso. She's stunning. I know incredible strength is my power, but I don't know if I have the strength to say goodbye to her.

She stops in front of me, tipping her head back to meet my eyes. I study the lines of her face, memorizing each feature that is unique to her—the luscious blue of her skin, the dark depths of her eyes, the full lips that have driven me mad countless times. It feels like just yesterday I was meeting her for the first time on our wedding day, my stomach in knots as I worried whether I'd be able to take care of her properly or not.

She loops her arms around my neck, and I wrap mine around her waist, hauling her off her feet and bringing her to my eye level. Her mouth finds mine, the kiss more gentle than the one we shared before we left Huxton's palace. This kiss feels more like a goodbye, and it makes my chest tight.

"Thank you," she sighs against my lips, and I tilt my head.

"What for?"

Her eyes are glittering as she leans her forehead against mine. "For loving me first," she whispers. "For trusting me first. For...everything."

I nearly choke around the knot of emotion building in my throat. I hold her tighter against me. "Don't do that," I say. "Please don't talk like you're saying goodbye."

"Never," she says, grazing her hand along my jaw before kissing me again. "I'm with you," she says, placing her free hand over the center of my chest.

I kiss her again, hard and long, doing my best to imprint the love I have for her on her soul. I send all the strength I can spare down our bond, and she trembles against me.

"Reaching the jump point," Talon says, his tone regretful but assertive.

I kiss her one last time before settling her on her feet. She backs up a few paces until she meets with Gessi near the ship's door. Talon hits a button and the door strains open, the sound of rushing air spilling in with a roar.

Gessi and Cari share a look, locking hands as they glance down at the sky below.

"Mate!" I shout over the roaring.

She glances over her shoulder, eyes crashing with mine.

"Come back to me," I demand, and she winks at me before the two lean forward, dropping out of the ship so fast my heart leaps to my throat.

Talon closes the door, silence filling the once loud space.

Blaize claps me on the back, leaving his hand there as Talon keeps the ship on its course toward the palace.

We can't even linger long enough to see if they land safely, since Talon's ship would be spotted if it stopped for that long.

I look at Blaize, and he presses his lips together, the same agony I feel mirrored in his eyes.

It's another thirty minutes before we land in the designated area the general directed us to—a wide expanse of beach on the tail end of a hill, the midnight ocean churning behind us. The sun is making its way toward setting, the general agreeing to meet just as the sun disappears behind the horizon.

"I don't like this location," I say as Talon, Blaize, and myself step off the ship to wait. Our armies are landing along the strip of beach behind us, at least a dozen ships filled with soldiers prepared to battle tonight.

"He'll have the high ground," Blaize finishes my thought, pointing toward the upper ridge.

"We knew that coming in," Talon says. "This is the general we're talking about. Nothing he does is ever clean or fair."

Blaize and I nod before the three of us approach the exiting soldiers, reminding them of their formations and instructing the team leaders to wait for our signal before attacking.

Adrenaline pulses through my veins as the sun hangs lower and lower in the sky, and just before it sinks, we hear the sounds of marching Shattered Isle guards in the distance.

"Here we go," Blaize whispers, reaching out his fist.

I bump it, a silent gesture of decades' worth of unflinching friendship.

Then I look at my brother, nodding at him to say all the things we can't voice. He clicks the buttons on his hands, his custom armor unfolding and wrapping itself around his body, leaving only his face uncovered for the negotiations.

The sounds of approaching soldiers grows louder and I take one second to send a prayer up for Tor, who leads one of the elite teams in the closest occupied territory. He'll join us soon, but for now, he's taking out the largest of the general's stationed soldiers so he can't call them in for reinforcements.

And then I see the general clear the view of the ridge, standing atop it and looking down at us like we're bugs to be crushed.

His teeth are razor sharp as he grins down at us, his arms folded over his chest as he waits for us to come to him.

I swallow my pride, motioning for the soldiers to stay behind as we previously instructed. Talon and Blaize follow right behind me as we scale the slight ridge, stopping only a handful of feet away from the general.

There are about five hundred guards behind him, all armed to the teeth as they await instruction.

Five hundred is a lot, but nearly as many as we were expecting. We have nine hundred of our own soldiers waiting below. Hope sneaks into my blood, but I make sure I keep my face even.

Neither of us speak first, waiting each other out in what I quickly realize is a losing battle. The general is too arrogant for that.

"General," I say, my voice stern.

"*King*," he corrects me, and I grind my teeth.

"King," I say. "Thank you for meeting with us to discuss terms of peace."

He arches his head back, looking down his nose at me, nothing but pure malicious, arrogance shaping his features.

"Huxton ensured me it would be worth my time," he says.

I nod, once again grateful for the Onyx City ruler. Not only did he house us and the victims of this war, but he was able to speak with the general and have the general actually listen. History is important with the Shattered Islers, and the general wasn't immune to the effects of a plea from one of his own.

"We want the suffering to end," I say, and it's not a lie. I want that more than anything. "Our two realms have bled enough at the hands of the other. It's time to end it for good."

He scans the area behind and below us like he's searching for something. "No false queens?"

Talon's fingers curl into fists, but he shakes his head. "With the volatile relationship between you and them," he says. "We figured negotiations for peace would go smoother if we left them in the Onyx City."

The general purses his lips. "Quite," he says, then cocks a brow at Talon. "*Prove* it."

"I don't have to prove shit to you," Talon snaps.

"I won't hear anything until you do."

"You son of a—"

"Talon," I snap, putting all the authority I possess into my tone. "Show him."

Talon glares at me, but brings up his arm and punches out a code until an image appears between us, the lights from his suit of armor illuminating Gessi and Cari.

They're sitting in Huxton's grand dining hall, looking weary as they sip tea.

The general steps closer to the image, his right-hand guard sticking close to his side as he examines the sight.

I try not to hold my breath, hoping Wynter's magic holds strong.

"I recognize the hall," the general says after a moment. "Huxton isn't one for change, is he?"

Relief uncoils my chest, but I don't let it show.

Talon rolls his eyes, punching the code again and killing the image.

"Peace comes at a high cost," the general says.

I narrow my gaze. "How high?"

"I was under the impression you had an offer to give," he says, irritation laced in his tone. "Speak it."

"In exchange for a cease-fire, including on your own people, we offer you full, legally binding rule over the Stone Realm."

His brow furrows as he looks over his shoulder at the guards waiting behind him. There are more Stone Realm people and Corters in the group than Shattered Islers. Guilt streaks through me, wondering how big of a hand we played in their role here. If we hadn't isolated them, would they still have run into his open arms? If our tentative peace between the Corters hadn't been so...tentative, would they have joined him? Is there anything we could have done to prevent this?

I squash the thoughts, knowing I could go on forever playing the what-if game and we don't have time for it.

"You don't hold rule over the Stone Realm," the general says. "They rule themselves, and they chose me. You have no legal grounds to offer it to me."

We knew that, of course, but we're trying to stall to give the girls as much time as possible. The longer we drag this out, the better their chances.

I press my lips together, shaking my head. "We can offer the Air Realm," I say. "It's the largest and most advanced realm within the All Plane, except for the royal city."

"And you'd grant me full political control over the territory?" he asks, and I nod. He considers for a while, glancing back at his army, then forward again. "What else?"

My lips part. "That's all we have to offer. And it should be more than enough to—"

"I'll tell you what is enough," he cuts me off, raising one of his hands to stop me from speaking.

It takes everything I have not to immediately stomp up to him and rip his spine out. That would trigger the battle sooner than my mate needs. I have to be patient.

"I want the Air Realm, the Corteran City, and the Earth Realm."

The fucking nerve of this male. "That's seventy-five percent of the All Plane," I say.

He shrugs. "That's the cost of peace."

"That's too fucking steep," Talon snaps, and the general cuts a glare his way. "No fucking way."

I hold up a hand to silence Talon, tilting my head in consideration. "You would cease all war efforts?" I ask.

"Yes," he says easily.

"Even among your own people?"

He nods.

"And you'd put it all in a binding contract?" I continue. "One that would give us the right to mow you down if you ever broke it?"

"Of course," he says, and I can see the delight dancing in his eyes.

He thinks he's won.

"Okay," I say, and I hate that even here, with the male responsible for poisoning my brother, for torturing my mate's best friend and traumatizing my mate her entire life, I still feel the bitter pang of the lie on my tongue.

"Steel," Talon hisses, but I stop him with a look.

"We need peace between our realms—"

"It won't be our realm if he's ruling more than half of it!" he fires back, stomping toward me. Blaize steps in his path, stopping his advance on me with his silver arm. "Take your hand off me," Talon growls, knocking Blaize's arm away.

The general laughs, a sticky, dark sound as he wags a finger in Blaize's direction. "On second thought," he says, and my stomach plummets. "I want him too."

"Excuse me?" Blaize snaps.

"I've heard stories of King Augustus's killer dog," he says. "The stories are legend, even here, about how well trained you are." He whistles. "Come here, boy." He pats his leg.

I move before thinking, barely stopping Blaize from rushing him. It takes all the strength I have to push him back.

"Stand down," I say, eying Blaize.

His eyes are murderous as he looks over my shoulder.

My friend is holding on by a fucking thread as he stares at the monster that tortured his mate.

"You'd be a welcomed replacement for my previous beasts," the general continues, glancing behind us. "Where are dear Varian and Crane?" he asks, sucking his teeth. "Remained behind with their female?" he shakes his head. "Such a shame. Such a waste." He looks at Blaize again. "You might be able to make up for their loss."

"Stand down," I whisper again, and Blaize shakes me off, but doesn't make another move toward the general.

"We're bartering with territories," I say. "You can have what we've discussed. Not him."

He arches a brow at me. "You're willing to give me entire territories with people in them, but *he* is where you draw the line?" His grin turns vicious. "And what if I asked for Cari?"

A low growl rumbles in my chest. "Don't."

He leans a little closer. "Or what?"

I clench my jaw, feeling the muscles threatening to snap. Anger blasts down the bond from Talon, the potency of it strong enough to make me shake with adrenaline.

"I think I will demand for her to be in the contract," he seethes. "We have unfinished business, her and I—" The sound of a guard racing up the ridge and over to him stops whatever he was about to say.

I take a calculated step back as the guard hurries to whisper something in his ear.

I spare a glance at Talon and Blaize, my heart in my fucking throat.

The general's eyes narrow as he waves the guard away, tsking us. "And you said you came here for peace." He shakes his head. "What a shame," he continues, nodding toward the guard on his right.

The guard nods back, rushing to the top of the ridge and firing one single blast into the sky.

The ground trembles beneath our feet, and I look over the ridge to see ten thousand more soldiers marching from where they were hidden behind a cove of rocks on the other side of the hill.

My blood turns to ice as I step back, standing between Blaize and Talon as we face the general.

"You didn't really think five hundred was all I had, did you?"

I swallow hard, my heart dropping to my stomach. We're severely outnumbered, but there is no going back now. I shift my feet, Talon slams his helmet over his face, and Blaize swings his silver arm in a readying circle as we all prepare for the oncoming impact.

One roar from Talon, and our own army storms up behind us as the general's comes over the ridge.

Everything slows down as I send a up a silent plea—
Cari, I hope we've given you enough time.

16

CARI

Gessi and I make our way through the tunnels like no time has passed at all. For all the tunnels haven't changed, we could be two younglings fueled with adrenaline as we break curfew in search of a few peaceful hours to ourselves.

But we're not heading away from the palace, we're diving into it.

A thick layer of dust falls over us as we remove the loose stone at the base of the palace floor in the main level dining hall, slowly lifting it to ensure we're alone.

Thankfully, there isn't a guard in sight. We're in luck, but that means they're all with the general who is currently talking to my mates...

Fuck, there is no win here.

Not yet.

I reach down and help Gessi up through the opening in the floor, carefully putting the stone back in place once we're both free of the tunnel.

We rise, keeping our feet light as we make our way

through grand dining hall, stopping short when we see a new structure acting as the room's center piece.

"Stars," Gessi says, covering her mouth as we both look up at the monstrosity.

It's a stone statue of the general's image, the towering height of it taking up half the room. He's standing on a hill of heads—the stones carved in the likeliness of his enemies.

"Well that inspires the people to follow him, I'm sure," I spit sarcastically.

Gess just shakes her head, and we do our best to skirt past the monstrosity and head silently out of the dining hall.

The palace hallways are eerily silent, only revving up the tension in my chest. The less people here means the more people lying in wait as my mates do their thing. We need to hurry. I flash Gessi a look that says as much, and she nods.

"We should check his rooms on the dungeon level, first," she whispers, and we head that direction.

We would've taken the tunnels that led directly to the dungeons, but I'd blown that cover the last time I snuck in here. That felt like eons ago, instead of the short time it's actually been.

Stars, when I think about it, so much has happened in such a short time—my marriage, falling for my mates, becoming queen of the All Plane, acquitting Lock of all his crimes, Gessi becoming queen of the Shattered Isle. It's all so much, but it's what we're fighting for, to protect what we love, both people and realm alike.

Thinking about Lock sends another wave of grief washing over me, the act of leaving him behind so much more significant in my soul than when I said goodbye to Tor, Talon, and Steel. All of them hurt like hell to do—the goodbye kisses and promises to stay safe—but at least I'd gotten that chance to do so with them. With Lock? All I had were dreams that I wasn't sure were real or just my desperation taking form in my mind.

Focus.

I have to focus.

We make it to the dungeons, turning down the hall where the general's rooms are. He has a massive bedchamber, a study, and a lab all to himself down here. I shiver against the dankness of the stone walls, my body remembering exactly what it's like to train down here for hours on end, the general barking in my ear, forcing Varian and Crane to fight me over and over and over again until we were all bleeding and battered.

I suck in a breath, steeling my nerves with the knowledge that he and father trained me to be a weapon, and I'm going to fucking show him just how well they did soon.

I fling my arm out when we round the corner near his lab, stopping Gessi. There are two guards posted outside the door, which makes hope flare in my blood. If they've been left behind, it's to protect something, and I sure as hell hope it's the All Cure.

Gessi and I share a look, nodding our heads in a countdown. Once we reach the end, we strike.

Ice and vine snap forward, slicing through the two guards with barely a sound.

They hit the floor, never knowing what hit them.

We nod, then hurry over their bodies to get into the lab. There isn't a hint of remorse coating my soul as we leave them behind—anyone who's aligned themselves so deeply with the general are beyond saving.

"Cari!" Gessi gasps as she heads deeper into the room. "It's here!"

My heart is in my throat as I chase after her, skidding to a stop before a large container with a soil-filled bottom.

Flowers bloom on thick green vines, jagged red and yellow petals looking like flames stretching from the base.

Stars, it's just how Gessi described it.

"They're protected," Gessi says, studying the container. She tries to touch the glass, but a searing shock nearly sends her to her feet.

"Shit," I hiss as I help steady her. "We need Talon."

"Or River," she says as we move on to search the rest of the space.

Right next to the container is another workstation, a sturdy table holding all manner of concoctions. It looks similar to Wynter's setup, only darker and more sinister. Gessi follows my attention, hissing when she spots a row of weaponized syringes.

"This is what he attacked you and your mates with?" I ask, leaning down to get a closer look.

"Yes," she says. "I'd recognize it anywhere."

As I draw nearer, it's like I can feel the effects without it even touching me. The powers in my blood tremble, urging me to run the opposite direction.

We move down the table, examining each vial of liquid. Most are the same color as the one Gessi recognizes, but there is one that stands out on the end, a purplish liquid encased in smaller syringes that could easily be concealed.

Somehow, either by instinct or circumstance, I know this is the poison he used against Lock. And next to the mixture are the dead remnants of the All Cure, as if someone had been dissecting it and extracting certain properties to make the poison before us.

"Gessi," I say, my mind whirling. "Fuck, look at this." I motion to the All Cure petals and vines all around the table, the tools scattered atop them. Then I glance at the purple poison. "He worked backward," I say, my heart racing with the realization.

"What?"

"He took the All Cure and worked backward," I say again, shaking my head. "He created the opposite of the All Cure," I continue, eyes wide as I note the color. It has a hint of that All Cure red swirling in the purplish hue. "Fuck. Of course. It would take nothing less to bring Lock down." Acid simmers in my veins. The general knew how powerful Lock was, knew it from the stories after we rescued Gessi and her mates. He knew he was the only real threat to his armies, and he created this specifically for him.

No wonder he hasn't woken up.

And will he ever?

With something this powerful?

My heart sinks to my stomach.

"There is one left out!" Gessi says, breathless as she scoops up a lone better left near the array of poisons in progress. She closes her eyes as her fingers brush the petals and vines, likely committing the elements to memory. "We can take it back and—"

"You two are really the dumbest bitches around, aren't you?" A guard spits the words at us as he enters the room, four more coming in behind him. "Coming back here? It's like you're begging to get hurt." He moves faster than we can register, brandishing a needle-thin whip that connects with Gessi's hand.

She yelps, the All Cure flower spills to the floor. She moves to scoop it up, but the guard cracks that whip again—

I slice the tip off with a blade of ice before it can connect with her face, stepping in front of her.

"Cari!" she chides me, my boots crunching on the All Cure petals. "You're crushing it!"

"Better it than your face," I say, and she blinks up at me, reality coming back to her eyes as more guards spill into the room. "Oh, wonderful," I say. "Four for each of us."

Gessi bolts to her feet, vines snaking their way from her palms.

"You think we want to get hurt?" I fire at the guard who is glaring at me for the death of his whip. I motion to him with a nod. "Why don't you come over here and find the fuck out?"

They rush us at full speed, and I grin.

Even better when they're in too much of a hurry to look at the ground.

I drop to one knee, my palms hitting the floor and spearing ice along its surface.

Each one goes down in a loud heap, sliding toward us from their rushed momentum.

Gessi's vines are barbed with milky thorns, snapping out like the whip from before, and I send spears of ice soaring right alongside them.

Seconds.

It takes us *seconds* to end every last one of them.

Our breaths are ragged as we take stock of what we've done, and then we smile at each other in victory.

But Gessi's smile drops when she looks down at the crushed petals, half frozen and destroyed from the quick battle. "No," she says, shaking her head as she rushes toward the container protecting the All Cure flowers again. "Maybe we can..." she hits the container with her vines, but sparks fly at the contact.

"We'll have to come back with Talon or River," I say, heart dropping to my stomach.

We knew it was here through. Knew it existed. That was something.

"If we hurry maybe we can—" Gessi stops abruptly when we hear the unmistakable rumble of a marching army on the ground above us.

Terror streaks through me. The ground is shaking above us, sending little bits of stone falling from the ceiling. The general's armies have been triggered.

Gessi and I share a look, dual panic flitting over each of our faces.

"It's started," I breathe, my heart split down the center. "We have to move," I say, grabbing her arm and hauling her out of the lab.

"The All Cure," she says, but runs behind me.

"Can't be accessed without help," I say. "Our mates are on the front line of this war." And I will not leave them to die.

We race through the palace, clearing it and the city streets easily with the lack of people as we head toward the meeting place.

"Fuck," Gessi breathes as we near the beach.

We both freeze.

We're on the wrong side at the tail end of the general's armies, and it's endless.

We're vastly outnumbered.

And all those numbers stand between us and our mates.

17

BLAIZE

F ucking. Hell.

I've seen some shit in my years, but this...

This is madness.

The general's armies comprised of Corters, Stone Realm soldiers, and Shattered Isle guards bear down on us like a swarm of angry ants whose anthill has just been kicked.

My head rings with the sound of battle cries, the ground trembling beneath our feet as they rush over the ridge toward us.

Talon blasts a single red flare into the sky, and our warriors react within a heartbeat. They race from behind us, their training kicking in as they crash against the enemy.

Adrenaline sharpens my senses, narrowing down my processing time to seconds.

Grab, snap, toss, grab.

I can only see the next enemy as they come at me, can only breathe around snapping necks and moving on to the next.

Each crack has me slipping into that cold darkness behind my assassin's mask. There is no room for compassion here, no room for hesitation or fear, not in a battle like this.

The bodies press in around me, grunts and groans as flesh hits flesh, blades clash against each other, and blasters crack through the air.

It's suffocating.

It's exhausting.

A Corter twice my size and donning Shattered Isle armor races toward me so fast I barely have time to drop the guard I just killed before he crashes against me.

The air blasts out of my lungs, making my eyes vibrate with the force of the impact as we hit the ground. Fuck, the Corter is massive, its weight nearly crushing as he pins me to the sandy earth. He draws a blade, hauling it back and jabbing it right toward my neck—

I block it with my tattooed arm, using its strength to stop the knife from tearing my throat open. My muscles shake as I fight to push the Corter off of me, rage pulsing like a drum in my blood.

Death is close, I can feel its greedy fingers clawing for my broken soul as the Corter gains the upper hand, pushing back against my defense, drawing that blade ever closer with a deep groan—

Something fast and hard slams into the Corter, sending it flying off of me.

Steel.

He slams a fist into the Corter's chest, and the monster goes limp beneath him. Steel spins around, offering me a blood-covered hand.

"I had it," I say, grabbing his hand.

"Try and stay on your feet next time," he says, helping haul me upward.

We're immediately hit by another wave of soldiers.

Instantly we fall into a battle rhythm, our backs pressed against each other as we fend off the enemies circling us.

Grab, snap, drop, repeat.

It feels like I'm breathing razor blades as we duck and dodge, swing and slam.

My muscles are shredded as I push and push and push my body beyond the boundaries it's become used to recently.

"Storm, check in!" Talon crashes against the sand right next to us, the blasters on his armor sending the remaining soldiers to the ground. We take a second to breathe as Talon continues to blast those coming for us.

"River's area is clear!" Storm's voice sounds over the speaker from Talon's tech armor. "Crane and Varian are still working on theirs. Tor has finished and is heading your way."

"Good," Talon responds, breathless as he surveys the battle around us.

Our soldiers are holding their own, but we're overwhelmed. The general's armies are fucking endless—

"Fuck," Storm says. "How does he have that many?"

He must be able to see through whatever tech Talon has on his suit.

"I can be there soon. I'm heading—"

"Don't," Talon orders. "Don't you dare come here, Storm. We need you to protect the All Plane in case..."

"In case nothing," Storm fires back at his friend. "You find a way to make it out of there!"

Talon cuts spins around, barely missing the attack of a Stone Realm soldier. They clash together in a battle of strength, and four more come racing for me and Steel.

We share a look as we prepare for the hit.

I focus only on those in front of me, forcing myself to not think about the thousands behind them that just keep on coming.

But for the first time ever, I don't see a way for us to survive this.

18

CARI

Working our way through the lines and lines of soldiers is slow going, like trying to push through a wall of tar.

Gessi and I are bleeding and gasping for breath as we cut down whoever steps in our way.

My emotions checked out minutes ago, my instincts switching solely to survive.

The collection of screams, grunts, and orders shouted across the soldiers rattles in my skull, overworking all my senses until almost everything sounds like a high-pitched whistle.

My ice sword cuts through a Stone Realm solider hell-bent on slicing off my arm, and he gurgles as he hits the ground. A clearing in the mass of fighting bodies opens up, and I scream for Gessi.

Her vines finish wrapping around two Corters as she looks at me. I point across the distance, toward a high ridge near the ocean.

"The general!" I call.

She narrows her gaze, and it widens when she spots him.

He's standing there, arms behind his back as he *watches* the battle rage around him. He doesn't lift a fucking finger to help his armies against us, the prick.

Gessi and I share a glance, and then we both sprint that direction. There are about a thousand bodies between us and him, but now that I've spotted him, there is nothing that is going to stop me.

We move quickly, leaping over lifeless bodies—both the general's and our own.

The more ground we cover, the more soldiers step into our path.

"Stars," I groan, ice spears soaring from my hands. "How many of you fuckers are there?"

"Too fucking many," Gessi says, breathless as she fights next to me. Every inch we gain we meet another half dozen guards who make it their sole mission to slow us down.

My limbs are exhausted and trembling as I swing a sword of ice back and forth, barely keeping the herd of the general's soldiers at bay. Gessi's vines snap and twist, barbs flying through the air as she tries to beat them back.

"At this rate," Gessi groans, wielding her vines around three soldiers while I blast four others with ice, "we'll be tapped out by the time we reach him!"

Fuck knows she's right, but there isn't a thing we can do about it. We have to go through the soldiers to get to him, to get to where our mates are on the other side. If we give now, we die.

"We need help," she says, and I block a dagger aimed for her neck with a wall of ice.

"We need a fucking miracle," I fire into the air.

"We need—"

An explosion of blaster fire and the roar of a sky ship cuts off Gessi's words. We both crouch to our knees, trying to take cover, but it only takes a few seconds to realize the ship isn't shooting at us.

The fire is hitting the soldiers in front of us, dusting them and creating a direct path to the general.

We both look up, and Gessi smiles as a massive obsidian beast soars through the air, landing so hard in front of her the ground shakes.

"Varian!" she wraps her arms around his monstrous form for a second only before pulling back. "You're *here*."

"Took us a bit to clear our territory," he says, his voice garbled from his shifted form.

A Corter runs full speed at our little group, and I draw ice into my palms, ready to send a spear right through his—

The Corter flies backward, an arrow sticking out of one eye.

Gessi whirls around just as Crane walks up behind her, giving her a fast embrace before nocking another arrow.

I arch a brow at Crane. "If you're here, who is flying the ship?"

Gessi and I both look up, watching as the ship sends blaster wave after blaster wave at those in front of us.

"River," Gessi says, a smile in her tone.

"He picked us up once he'd cleared his territory," Crane explains, firing off another arrow and nocking another.

A group of the general's soldiers stops coming for our group, instead directing their blasters toward the ship above us. River maneuvers away from it, twisting and weaving before returning fire.

Another wave crashes toward us, Corters and Stone Realm alike.

Varian steps in front of Gessi and me, Crane following suit.

"Go," Varian yells over his shoulder. "We'll handle them."

Gessi looks longingly at her mates, torn between standing to fight with them, and rushing toward the general to finish this.

I spare her a glance before racing down the path River created for us. She can stay with her mates if she wants—mine are all on the other side of the general, and I have to get to them.

The sand beneath my feet gives as I fly down the path, the air kissing my sweat-and-blood-soaked skin as I propel myself faster and farther.

I can see him clearly now, pacing along the upper ridge as he watches the carnage unfold. He's so close I can make out the delight in his eyes. He's enjoying every bit of this.

The sky opens up, a massive bolt of lightning striking the ground just beyond the general, loud and quick enough to make him flinch.

My smile widens as I keep running—Tor is here.

Talon and Steel are down there somewhere, just over the ridge, fighting too.

The only one missing is Lock.

Rage pulses in my blood, pushing me harder toward the male responsible for my missing mate.

Twenty feet.

That's all that separates me from him.

My heart races, my lungs tight and raw as I go faster, ice ready and arms drawn back as I shape a spear. His leg, I'm aiming for his leg. I want to take him down, but not kill him. He doesn't deserve a fast, easy death. He deserves to suffer.

I send the spear flying.

The general whirls around, spotting me before he dodges out of the way and—

Fucking *disappears*.

"Coward!" I roar, sending a wave of snow crashing over the ridge, the white flakes falling over his invisible shape. "Face me!"

He shakes off the snow, disappearing again. I brace myself, trying to listen for his footsteps, but the battle raging all around us is too damn loud.

Another bolt of lightning strikes the beach below, drawing my attention.

"Tor," I breathe his name, spotting him fighting next to Talon below. Steel is down there too, Blaize at his side as they fight and fight and fight.

Stars, there are so many fucking soldiers down there—the general's and ours.

Something hard cracks against my shin, sending me dropping forward. My spine barks as something hits me from behind, knocking the air out of my lungs. I hurry to my feet, throwing out my palms as I send another flurry of snow soaring all around me.

There.

He's to my left, rushing toward me in a nearly-invisible blur of white. I swing out for him, barely clipping him with an icy fist as he flies past me, kicking my feet out from beneath me again.

"Bastard!" I hiss, clambering to my feet. My muscles feel like worn-out rubber, my thighs shaking as I dig my heels in for balance. "Show yourself, you fucking coward!"

Something grips me from behind, a muscled arm wrapping around my throat. I flail against it, swinging my legs in an effort to throw him off.

He doesn't budge.

"It's not cowardly to use the powers you have," the general says, his voice at my ear. "I thought I taught *you* of all people that."

I can't breathe.

He's crushing my throat.

"I'm not going to kill you, sweet princess," he says, his hold tightening. "I'm going to break you. Piece by piece, until there is nothing left but the weapon I deserve. Until you're a shell who kills on command. Until *you* are what the Shattered Isle and All Plane fear. And I'll be at the helm of it, ruling unchecked over all."

No, no, no.

I struggle against him, but can't shake him off.

I'm a youngling again who failed a task and he's punishing me for it. He'll punish my friends next.

I can see my mates fighting below as my vision darkens around the edges, my heart slowing. Steel's eyes meet mine for a second in time, and I hear him scream something up at me.

Steel.

Talon.

Tor.

And Lock...Stars, Lock.

The general is trying to take everything from me.

And I'm about to fucking let him.

I curse my body, curse the exhaustion clinging to it and my powers, and dig deep. I reach up with serrated ice claws and slice along his grip.

He roars, instantly releasing me.

I gasp for breath, taking in deep lungfuls as my head clears. I whirl around.

The general stands before me, fully visible and bleeding. He's looking at the wound with a shocked expression I've never seen before. He's looking at *me* like he's never seen me before.

He bares his razor-sharp teeth at me. "First order of business in breaking you," he says, shifting on his feet. "Is watching me tear your mates to pieces."

Ice daggers form in my hands. "Let's finish this."

19

GESSI

C ari is racing away from us before I can even process what Varian is saying.

And before I can think or move, another three Corters race toward us. I wield my vines, snapping them like whips of barbed steel as the soldiers approach. My power feels watery in my veins, but I can't stop fighting. Especially when my mates are right here, fighting for their lives next to me.

"Gess," Varian practically growls at me as he elongates his arms, crushing enemy after enemy with them. "I said *go*!"

"I can't leave you two here!" I fire back, breathless. At least River is in the sky, somewhat safe from the overwhelming amount of enemies all around us. And Blaize, stars, I hope he's faring better on his beach position with Steel and Talon.

"You can!" Crane yells over his shoulder, firing arrow after arrow at the approaching soldiers.

Varian stomps toward me, looking down at me from all

ten feet of his shifted form. "You and Cari have to end this," he says. "We'll be right behind you. Go!"

I swallow hard, tears filling the backs of my eyes as I nod at both of them before turning around and sprinting down the path River so graciously afforded us.

They're right.

Of course, I know they're right.

The general needs to die by my hand or Cari's and no other. He's delivered so many horrendous tortures to the two of us over the years...it *has* to be us.

"Let's finish this." Cari's voice reaches me over the sounds of the battle raging around me just as I clear the ridge, finding her facing off against the general.

They both look battered, but Cari is faring much worse than him. She's been fighting as long as I have while the general has done nothing but stand and watch.

He rushes toward her, advancing with the precision of a viper, but she dodges every hit. I've seen her face him numerous times in the training ring, and she's always lost.

But he's never fought us together.

He lands a blow to her stomach, and Cari doubles over, her ice daggers flying from her hands.

"Tragic little thing, aren't you?" he seethes, gripping her chin right before he punches her across the face.

Fuck, I climb higher, faster.

"You were supposed to be the weapon we always wanted." He shakes his head, blocking her weak attempt at retaliation. "Such a waste." He slides his hands up her face, his thumbs poised over her eyes—

I snap a vine around his ankle and yank him back.

He falls hard on his stomach, his chin bouncing off the sand.

Cari breathes deep, shaking off the stun of the hits, and

smiles at me. Her teeth are lined in blue, her blood dribbling down the corner of her mouth.

But the general is bleeding too, and that's enough for me.

I draw my power inward, dragging him toward me—

He flips over, slicing through my vine with his razor sharp teeth, freeing himself from my grasp.

"Ah, my precious little flower," he says, moving so he can see us both. I'm to his right, Cari to his left, and we're both advancing. "Come back to play?"

The scars along my body prickle at his voice, memories flooding me. Every torture, every hurt, every mental manipulation.

"Come to *kill*," I correct him, adrenaline racing through my veins.

I spare a glance to Cari, who meets my eyes with a determination I can practically feel in my bones.

"I'm so lucky," he says, drawing our attention as he raises his hands, a knife poised in each one, "to have the two of you here. Both my lovely girls. It's poetic, that you'll meet your end together."

We move as one, both of us rushing him with all the strength we have left.

Cari with her ice, me with my vines. We snap and lash out, swinging and clawing—

He dodges and blocks us, his moves quick like a striking snake. He has years and years of experience on us, not to mention the advantage of knowing how we fight, but that doesn't stop us.

Neither does the exhaustion stretching wide in my body, the adrenaline doing its best to counteract it, to keep me going, keep me alive.

All we need is one good move.

One good hit to gain the upper hand, then the two of us can take him down.

But we have to manage to strike him first.

He blinks in and out of sight, throwing off my senses as he disappears only to appear behind me and I spin just as he swipes his blade at my face—

It sinks into a wall of ice, and he growls at the way his hand bounces off of it.

Cari pushes forward, chasing him with snow as he goes invisible again, the white flakes giving us only glimpses of where the prick is as he hops around us.

I track the moves, my heart pounding in my chest as rage roars in my mind.

He has to die.

He *has* to.

I spot his intended move, a quick fake to the left, only to go right—

I lash out, wrapping a vine around his invisible throat, hauling him to me.

He flickers into sight, eyes wide as I reel him in, a needle-sharp blade of wood forming in my free hand. I draw it back, my muscles flexing for the strike—

A white-hot sear flares at my hip, and I look down as I stumble back.

"Gessi!" I hear Blaize screaming from somewhere close, but I can't see him.

I can only see the knife sunk into the flesh near my hip, can only see the general's malicious grin as my vines slip away from his neck.

"Such a pretty little flower," he says, jerking the knife out of me. "Look at how you bleed."

"No," Cari gasps, racing up behind him.

My head is spinning as I fall to the ground, my mind whirring.

From an angle, I can see Blaize rushing up the ridge, someone chasing after him. But my vision goes blurry right before it goes wholly black.

CARI

"N o," I gasp as I see Gessi fall to her side, her head heavy against the sand as she covers her wound with her hands.

Blaize is racing up the hill behind me, screaming Gessi's name like he can feel the wound himself, but I can't see anything beyond the general.

Beyond his smile.

He's *smiling* as he looks down at my best friend, bleeding on the sand.

"You're dead," I say, hurling a massive ice blade at his back, no longer caring about the suffering he deserves.

He spins around, catching my ice sword right before it connects with his chest. He tilts his head, tsking me as his eyes light up. He chucks the sword back at me with a deadly force, and I dodge out of the way—

A sickening *thwack* sound erupts behind me, followed by a groan.

I whirl around, eyes widening.

Steel is behind me.

And my ice sword is in the center of his chest.

CARI

"Steel," I whisper his name, my mind unable to understand what it's seeing.

Steel drops to his knees, his hands shaking around the ice blade in his chest.

Blaize is screaming as he unleashes himself on the general behind me.

I rush to Steel, who falls against me as we both hit the ground, him half in my lap as I look down at him.

"You're okay," I say, tears rolling down my cheeks. "You're fine."

He's fine. He's so damn strong. He has to be okay.

He visibly swallows, and his normal searing blue eyes are too light a blue as he looks up at me. "I love..." His voice is too weak.

I shake my head, cringing against the pain flaring down the bond between us. I can feel him, feel how drained he is from the battle. His powers are weak, and this...this wound is...

I can't say it.

I can't think it.

"Please," I beg him. "Stay with me. Steel," I cry his name. "Stay with me."

"Love," he breathes the word and his eyes fall shut.

"No!" I run my hands over his chest, around the blade I'm too scared to take out. My fingers are instantly covered in his blood. "Steel. Wake up! Wake up!"

He doesn't stir.

My *heart*.

Steel is my heart. He's the one who loved me first.

I throw my head back, roaring at the sky as I feel the bond between us waning.

It's dying.

Our bond is dying.

Instinct takes over. I feel nothing but icy rage as I gently move out from under Steel, climbing to my feet.

My power rages, thrashing inside my blood, as if it refuses to believe what's happening.

"Move," I order, my voice unrecognizable and cold. "Move, Blaize. *Now*."

Blaize and the general are fighting, an endless frenzy of movement.

He doesn't move.

He doesn't stop lashing out.

And I don't have it in me to care.

I *erupt*.

Ice spears from every inch of my body in a shockwave that knocks both of them on their ass. Blaize rolls to his feet, instantly leaping over Gessi who still lies unconscious on the ground.

The general doesn't make it to his feet.

Not while I have ice chains snaking around his ankles and wrists, holding him in place as I stalk toward him.

First Lock.

Now Steel.

I stand over him, controlling ice that is beyond cold, beyond brutal, beyond rage. My powers and I are one— numb and raw and endless.

I tilt my head, creating massive snakes of ice that slither around him, curling around his torso, squeezing so tight he gasps for breath.

I lean down, drawing my face closer to his, and relish as he shudders in fear.

"You wanted a weapon," I whisper, curling my fingers as a new ice snake slithers its way up his chest, his throat, and hovers over his mouth. "You fucking got it."

I clench my fingers into a fist, the ice snake shooting down his mouth before violently bursting out of his chest, the general's still beating heart in its mouth.

Silence fills my head, fills my soul, as I take that heart in my hand, freezing it until it crumbles in a mess of broken ice at my feet. Panic beats at the numb barriers I hold it at bay with.

Panic.

And so much fucking despair.

I can't turn around. I can't see him lying there—

"Cari," Gessi's voice is weak, but strong enough that I snap out of myself. "Take me to him, Blaize."

I turn to her, relief at seeing her alive, seeing her awake. She's clutching that wound, but it's no longer bleeding. She's sewn it up with her power—

"You're weak," Blaize says, his voice wrecked, his eyes tear-filled.

"Take me to him, *now*." Gessi demands, and Blaize lifts her, carrying her toward...

Toward Steel.

My heart shatters at the sight of him there.

"Gessi, no!" I scream as she rips the sword from his chest. I race toward her, sinking to my knees as my hands fly to cover the wound.

"Cari," she snaps, forcing me to look at her. She holds out her hands, and a flower blooms between them.

A beautiful flower that looks like the embodiment of flame.

The All Cure flower.

The few petals she held in the palace must've been enough for her to imprint it to memory.

I move my hands away, shock filling every inch of me as she wields her power, stripping the flower down to its base until a liquid seeps from the petals and vines and drips over Steel's wound.

"Please work," Blaize whispers, eyes strained as he looks at Steel. "Come on, Steel. Please."

Pain radiates down my body. I can feel Steel's bond, but it's weak, barely a wisp of life. I shake my head, tears streaming down my cheeks. "We're too late," I cry.

The ground shakes beneath us.

"Fuck," Blaize snaps, standing up to survey behind us.

I follow him, my body still on survival mode.

The last wave is gaining ground and heading straight for us.

"Steel!" Talon's voice is a broken scream behind me. I rush toward him, watching the devastation play out on his face. Tor holds him back as Gessi still tries and tries to revive him.

We're broken.

We're outnumbered.

Our soldiers are fighting for their lives in all directions.

And the sand is coated in so much blood.

"The general is dead," I say. "But he's still winning."

"Look," Gessi says, and I drag my eyes to her. She points to Steel's chest. The wound is sealed, but he's...he's not moving. He's not waking up.

"I can't do this anymore. I can't keep losing..." I say, feeling like an empty shell. "I can't...I can't..."

First Lock.

Now Steel.

"You can and you will." Gessi's hands are on my face as she forces me to look into her green eyes.

When did she move?

When did I fall to my knees?

Talon and Tor are behind her, already fighting as the final wave of soldiers arrive. Lightning snaps through the air, followed by blaster fire from Talon's armor.

"Cari!" Gessi snaps, and I blink at her. "You will fight. You will finish this. You're the All Plane queen. Your people need you. Talon and Tor need you. *I* need you! Please. We can't do this alone."

I tremble in her embrace as something strong and unending bursts inside me. I don't know if it's my powers giving me one last boost, one last wave of power, but I take it, cling to it, and nod at my friend.

"I'm with you," I say, despite feeling completely broken inside. We stand together, and she races to Blaize's side, Varian and Crane clearing the ridge with the rest of the general's armies a minute behind them. "I'm with you," I say again, knowing that Talon and Tor will be next if I give up. If I let myself crumble.

Later. I can fall apart later.

Right now, my family needs me.

River flies overhead in the sky ship, firing at a good section of the enemy forces climbing up the ridge toward us.

Our armies are meeting the wave surrounding the ridge, what's left of them pushing back with all they can.

"We promised you a reckoning!" I yell at the approaching wave, taking a defensive stance in front of Steel's body. "Now you're going to get one."

The soldiers fly over the ridge, hitting each of us head-on.

I'm quickly facing seven of the biggest Stone Realm soldiers I've ever seen, each one armed to the teeth with blades.

"An All Plane king's head," the one in the middle spits. "It will make a fine centerpiece for my table." He grins at his buddies. "As will your pretty chest." He points at me with his blade, and I flick my wrists, nearly imperceptible shards of ice flying forward so fast he doesn't have time to block them.

His head slides from his body before it hits the ground.

I meet the other six's eyes, creating another sword of ice as I point it at them. "You'll have to cut me down to get to him."

They roar as a group, rushing me—

Hit, block, stab, slice.

My arms are shredded, my thighs shaking.

My power is waning even as I push back the six. Even as I cut each of them down until Steel is surrounded by a pile of body parts.

More come to take their place.

Blaize and Gessi and Varian and Crane are overrun too.

Talon is on the ground several yards away, three Corters atop him as he tries to fight them off.

Tor is growling, his lightning crackling in waves and waves as more and more keep coming over the ridge.

I grip the sword in my hand, creating another one in my free one as a group of ten head straight for me.

I'm hanging on by a thread, but I hold up my swords.

We have seconds left before we're completely overtaken. I can see it in the strength the enemies have, the numbers they hold. I can smell it in the blood that hangs in the air.

At least when I die here, I'll die by my mates, my family.

And in the end, I guess that's all I can really ask for.

22

CARI

I close my eyes and swing.

That's all I can do. A lifetime of assassin training is no match for the sheer exhaustion draining my strength, my powers.

I slice my sword through the air as the group surrounds me, suffocates me. I'm swinging and swinging, cutting into anything that's close enough to reach.

Four of them slam into me, knocking the blades from my hands. My spine smacks into the sand, my head bouncing from the impact. My mind rattles, but my body keeps fighting, keeps reaching for a power that is completely burned out in my veins.

I kick and punch and scream, but I can't get up.

They're too heavy.

Their punches are too hard.

I can feel myself slipping, feel the mental grip I have on my consciousness waning.

Turning my head, I see Steel. They haven't touched him.

Good.

That is good—

A fist slams into the side of my head, and my entire body goes limp.

Shadows envelop the world.

Darkness is something I've always welcomed, but I can't help but fight the grip of death now.

My mates...

They need me.

I need them.

But I'm so cold, so tired. And death is here, wrapping me in a blanket of darkness that is almost soft to the touch, almost loving as it caresses the edges of my skin.

Awareness ripples down my soul, down my bond.

The smell of snow and stars invigorates me as it spears from the shadows—

Shadows.

Not death.

My death.

Adrenaline floods my body as realization shakes my mental awareness. Dust falls around me, the Corters who were just atop me no longer there.

I scramble to sit up, eyes wide as I watch the darkness sweep over the enemy forces in a crashing wave that leaves nothing but dust in its wake.

Talon rises to his knees, shaking his head.

Tor is laughing, hollering at the shadows swooping across the battlefield.

Blaize, Varian, and Crane are forming a protective barrier around Gessi.

And then the world grows quiet as those shadows pull into themselves, folding over and over again as it draws back and back, until it's nothing but a male-sized shape swirling before me.

"*Lock*," I cry out, my knees buckling as the shadows clear

from his body. They still cling to his eyes, his pupils blown out and wide as he strides toward me, dropping to his knees as he pulls me into his arms. "How?" I cry, running my hands over his face, his chest, and back up again.

He slams his mouth to mine, kissing me in a dangerous, claiming kiss that awakens every inch of my soul, my body, before he draws back, looking at me with blue-green eyes. "Is that real enough for you, darling?"

My lips part, brow furrowing. "It was real?"

"You found me," he says. "You helped me shake the poison's hold. I tried to do it alone, but I couldn't. I needed *you*."

"You have me," I breathe the words as I fall against him. "You've always had me."

He clings to me, kissing me over and over again before drawing me to my feet, looking down at the remnants of the general.

"He deserved it," I say.

"Such a cruel, creative little mate," Lock says.

"Took you long enough," Talon says from behind us, and I shift out of the way as he wraps Lock in a fierce hug.

"Unconsciousness can do that," Lock says, moving out of Talon's embrace and into Tor's. "Where is—"

A low groan sounds from behind us, and I spin around, heart in my throat. Steel is groaning as he shifts up to his elbows, brow pinched as he glances around. "Did we get him?"

A half-laugh half-cry rips out of me as I race over to him, throwing my arms around his neck. "I thought I lost you," I whisper as he holds me against his chest.

He presses his cheek against the top of my head. "Never," he says. "Never again."

I blow out a breath, helping him to his feet. I barely have

time to move before Blaize slams into him, hugging him as he claps his back. "Don't you ever fucking do that to me again," he says. "Or I'll kill you."

Steel laughs, hugging him back.

I head to Gessi, wrapping my arms around her. "You saved my mate," I say, gratitude dripping from my tone. "I can never thank you enough."

She waves me off as we separate, Varian and Crane coming over to hug me too. "Your mate just saved all our lives," she says, glancing at Lock. "I think we're even."

We're not, but I can't help but smile.

I feel like I barely have the strength to stand...but we're all standing. That's all that matters.

Lock moves back to me, sliding his arm around my waist. "Talon," he says, nodding toward him. "Looks like you have quite a lot of soldiers who are confused."

Talon, Tor, and Steel glance toward the ocean where there are indeed a ton of soldiers looking around each other and the dust at their feet.

"The kingly thing to do would be to explain it to them," Lock continues.

"The people of the Shattered Isle will be terrified," Gessi says, looking to Crane and Varian and then Blaize. "We'll need to tell them they're safe."

"Yes," Lock says, then sweeps an arm beneath my knees, scooping me off my feet and cradling me to his chest. I yelp in surprise, but fling my arms around his neck. "That's the royal thing to do."

Talon cocks a brow at him. "You're a king too," he says. "You can help—"

"I just did," Lock cuts him off. "Decimated an entire army, remember?"

Tor barks out a laugh. Talon shakes his head. Steel is already heading toward the soldiers on the beach.

"Besides..." Lock looks down at me, eyes like liquid fire. Shadows swirl around his ankles, working their way up his long legs until they tickle my hips. "I've always been more of a villain anyway." He winks at Talon before his shadows completely engulf us.

23

GESSI

"I think it's safe to say the people are finally settling back in," River says as we walk through the palace halls.

"There are many still dealing with the trauma the general inflicted," I say as we round a corner.

It's been a month since we defeated the general and his armies on the battlefield, and while the survivors are back in their homes and territories, living free, there is still much to do to heal the wounds the general inflicted.

"They're alive," Varian barks from behind me. "And they're free. Everything else—like healing—will come with time."

I sigh, nodding. We turn into one of Varian's favorite areas in the palace, a lounge room with cushions all along the floor, a wide-open balcony with its doors open to let the night in, and a crackling hearth on the farthest wall.

It's been a long night.

A long month.

But we're making progress. Loads of it, but I can't help feeling like it's not enough.

"You saw how ecstatic the people were earlier," Crane says as he drops his bow and arrows at a little weapons station in the corner. River does the same with his belt of gadgets. "They love you. They're grateful for you."

"I hope I can continue to earn those feelings," I say, taking off my crown and setting it on a little table near a wooden cart filled with all manner of liquor.

"You will," Blaize says, settling on a cushion next to me while Varian heads to the wooden cart to mix us all drinks.

We haven't even tried to relax since winning the battle, since ending the war. But tonight...tonight feels safe in a way it hasn't in months.

"Have you spoken to Cari?" Varian asks as he hands me a drink, then continues passing them out to River, Crane, and Blaize.

I take a quick sip of the citrusy concoction, letting it slide down my throat before taking a much-needed deep breath.

We're safe.

The Shattered Isle is safe.

My mates are here and alive and well.

I've had to repeat this to myself more times than I can count.

"Yes," I finally answer Varian after he settles in a spot across from me. River takes my left side, Crane content on a corner cushion that gives him the best view of all four of us. "They're still working out the Stone Realm situation," I continue. "There were innocent people in that community. Talon has Storm heading up investigations on who is loyal and who isn't, and they're all working toward a new peace treaty where they'll officially bring the Stone Realm back into the All Plane."

Blaize shakes his head, taking a huge gulp of his drink.

"What?" I ask.

"The Stone Realm has been at odds with the All Plane for decades," Blaize answers before shrugging. "I hope they know what they're doing."

I can't help but agree, though I know in these new times after war, there has to be bridges built between those who were excluded before. It's a new era, one I hope we can maintain for as long as possible.

As we sip our drinks, each minute ticking by relaxing us a little more, I look at my mates and see a future—a glittering future filled with possibilities. It's not some great revelation, but it strikes me to the core. Since mating them, I haven't had a chance to look past the war, but now that it's over, now that we've garnered some peace...I can see it.

I see endless nights of laughter and love with River.

I see brilliant moments of brutal pleasure with Blaize.

I see thrilling adventures with Varian.

I see sleepless nights spent reminiscing and healing with Crane.

And I see a queendom whose people are prosperous and happy, our allies in the All Plane much the same.

Excitement floods my veins, a sort of intoxicating hope that brings a smile to my lips.

Crane arches a brow at me, but he smiles softly.

"Whatever you're thinking," River says, trailing a finger down the side of my bare arm. "Keep thinking it. That smile is *everything*."

I look at each of them, my heart so full I can barely breathe. "You," I say to all of them. "I'm thinking of each of you. Of the future we can have now."

Varian's smile is wholly beast-like as he tilts his head, eyes roaming over me. My blood spikes with heat with just that look, and there is a collective gasp between them, all of them feeling it down our bonds.

"What about the immediate future?" Varian asks, wetting his lips as he shifts on the cushions, setting his empty drink on a little nearby table. "You have any thoughts on that, love?"

Stars, do I.

My eyes flicker from him, to River, to Blaize, to Crane, and back to Varian. So many options, so many delicious choices. How did I get so lucky?

A warm shiver races over my skin as Varian stalks closer on his hands and knees, stopping when his lips are just a breath away from mine. "Tell us," he says, branding me with a quick kiss. "Tell us what you want."

My pulse takes off as River moves behind me, placing tender kisses along my neck. "I want..." I gasp when Varian kisses me again, stealing my breath and making my head spin.

"You want..." Varian says against my mouth.

"I want each of you," I answer, heart racing. I look behind Varian, at Blaize and Crane, who have moved closer. "I want you to use me to make yourselves feel good."

Varian groans, and River shudders behind me.

"I think we can manage that, my queen," River says, kissing the shell of my ear. "Right?" he asks the group, and they don't need to verbalize the agreement, I can feel it radiating down our bonds—pure passion and love and need.

"Dibs on first," Varian says, his voice leaving no room for argument. He wraps a strong arm around my waist, hauling me against him until I'm straddling his lap, my dress flowing out around us. "Let's see how badly you need it, love," he says, spearing his hand beneath my dress. He shifts my lacy underwear to the side, and growls when he finds my heat. "Stars, love," he groans, rubbing his fingers through me. "You're so slick."

I tremble at his touch, wrapping my arms around his neck and slanting my mouth over his. He kisses me hungrily, teasing me with his fingers until I rock against his hand.

Varian draws his mouth from mine, a smirk on his full lips. "River," he says, motioning River over. "Our mate's breasts need attention."

I throw my head back as River slides behind me again, his hands reaching around to cup my breasts. A moan escapes my lips as he moves the fabric of my dress until my chest is exposed, the cool air hissing against my heated skin. I turn my head against River's chest, my eyes meeting Crane's and then Blaize's a few feet away.

They're both watching patiently, fire in their eyes, and stars, it does things to my body. Knowing they're watching River and Varian's every kiss, every touch, is thrilling in a way I'll never tire of.

Varian swipes his thumb over my aching clit, and I gasp, jerking against his touch, bringing my attention right back to him. He grins, nipping my bottom lip before taking his hand away. I whimper at the loss of his touch.

"Lean her back," he says, and River immediately complies, shifting until I'm laying back against River's strong chest, his hands still teasing my nipples until my breasts are heavy and aching.

I watch as Varian moves to his knees, his hands pushing my dress up to my waist before he parts my thighs. His eyes glow with his partial shift, and he grins at me before dipping his head between my thighs.

"Varian!" I gasp as I feel his sharp teeth graze the sensitive skin of my thigh. Something rips, and he comes back with my lace between his teeth.

He tosses it to the side, giving me a peek of that elongated tongue before he dives between my legs again—

"Stars," I moan, arching back against River as Varian slides his tongue up my slit. I reach up, clinging to River as Varian laps at me over and over again, working me up so fast and so hard I see stars.

Varian spears his tongue inside me, thrusting it in and out between teasing my swollen clit, all the while River kisses my neck and shoulders, working my breasts between his hands.

"How does she taste?" River asks, his cock rock hard as it presses against my ass.

"Divine," Varian growls against my flesh, making me gasp. "Fucking divine."

My body tightens as he eats at me, the blood in my veins turning into liquid fire. Stars, his tongue, River's hands...it's a wonderful combination. I rock my hips into Varian's mouth, giving in to the instincts driving my body toward the edge.

Varian groans, his hands strong as they clutch my hips, helping propel me against him.

"Varian," I moan. "Please."

"Look at those manners," Blaize says across the room, and I draw my hazy eyes to him.

Stars, he's taken his shirt and pants off, leaving him only in his black underwear that shows off exactly how much he's enjoying the show.

"Let her come, Varian," Blaize says in that demanding tone of his that sends fire streaking through me.

Varian flattens his tongue against my aching clit right before sucking it into his mouth—

I convulse, my orgasm rocking through me in a wave of pleasure that tingles down my spine. My thighs tighten around his head as I keep coming, my body shaking with delight as electricity crackles though me.

"Mmm," Varian groans, pulling back to lick his lips only after he's worked me down.

I'm limp against River, but Varian wastes no time in shedding his clothes and settling himself between my thighs. River shifts behind me, the two of them moving me around like their own personal doll as he takes his pants off.

"Give me a taste," River says, and I go wholly liquid as Varian grins, leaning over me to kiss River. It's passionate and fierce and makes me shiver as I watch them. "Fuck," River groans as Varian draws back, his lips grazing over my exposed breasts. "You're so delicious, my queen."

"Play with her ass," Varian says, and River moves behind me, dragging his hard cock down the seam of my ass.

I jerk against the touch, which has Varian's cock gliding through my wetness. He groans, moving until his tip is lined up with my entrance. "You're on fire, love," he says, sliding his cock through my wetness until he's drenched in it. He moves, dragging it lower until he meets with River, who moves aside to allow him to soak my tight hole.

"Stars," I groan, one hand digging into Varian's shoulder, the other clinging to River's muscled forearm wrapped around my torso.

"Together," River says, and Varian nods, the two communicating over and behind me.

They each inch into me at the same time, tearing a throaty gasp from my lips. I relax, allowing River to inch in just as Varian bottoms out inside me, until they're both filling me so much I can barely breathe from the intensity of it.

But somehow, I still want *more*.

They fall into a rhythm that has my muscles loosening

and tightening all at the same time. Each thrust, each touch, each graze of their lips along my skin has me winding up so damn tight I feel like I'll snap any minute.

More, more, more.

I roll my head to the side, eyes finding Blaize first. "Blaize," I say on the end of a moan. "Come here," I beg him, and he smirks as he gets closer.

He rakes his silver fingers through my hair, tight enough to send delicious spirals of pain down my spine.

Varian groans as I clench around him in reaction to Blaize, River shuddering behind me as he maintains his pace.

"Need me to fuck that pretty mouth of yours?" Blaize asks, reading my mind.

"Please," I beg, parting my lips for him.

Blaize cocks a brow down at me as he drags his cock over my mouth, his smooth head hot and firm against my lips. I flick out my tongue, moaning at the taste of him—

He shoves his cock into my mouth so fast I gasp, my pussy fluttering as Varian and River fuck me. Stars, he tastes like a dream as he pulls out and thrusts in again. I shiver with how full I am, my mates claiming every inch of me and more.

I keep my mouth open and my body as loose as possible as they have their way with me, each stroke, thrust, and caress swirling a white-hot tension inside me. Over and over again, they fuck all parts of me, driving my body over the edge and straight into a place where I'm nothing but sensation. Everything feels so damn good—all slick and hot, the bonds between us vibrating with pleasure as they take and take and take from me.

Blaize ups his pace, and Varian and River follow, as if they can all feel my pleasure building to a crescendo.

I can't think, can't breathe around the feel of them.

And then I see Crane, slowly stalking the edge of the cushions, his eyes molten as he watches. The sight is enough to have my veins fill with liquid gold, and then Varian grinds against me while bottoming out—

I moan around Blaize's cock, my fingers digging into Varian and River as I fly apart, shattering completely into a million pieces. Little explosions erupt down my spine, Varian and River's thrusting driving me from one swoop of pleasure right into another one, until my head is spinning with how much pleasure they rip from my body.

"You want it, mate?" Blaize groans the question, his fingers tight in my hair as he pumps into my mouth.

I moan my consent, and he growls, spilling into my mouth and down my throat. My eyes water from the size of him, but I swallow him down, relishing the taste of him as he gently slides out of my mouth—

Varian growls, pounding into me with a ferocity that has River going still, allowing Varian's momentum to drive all three of us until they both come inside me.

I'm shaking, breathless, and sensitive as they rock through the aftershocks—

"My turn," Crane says, and I barely have time to blink before Varian and River are sliding out of me and Crane's arms haul me up and away from the group. My feet don't even touch the floor as he walks us to the closest wall.

I lock my ankles around his back, my entire body on fire as he thrusts into me, my pussy still drenched with Varian's come. My spine presses against the wall, but Crane slides a strong arm beneath my ass, holding me up as he fucks me.

His eyes are on mine, not once breaking as he pounds into me over and over again with a relentless energy that makes every nerve in my body spark to life all over again. I fling my arms around his neck, clinging to him as he drives into me, grinding against me in sure strokes that have flames licking every inch of my skin.

"Crane," I gasp, my mind losing focus as he turns me into nothing but a tight string of need. "Stars, *Crane*. I'm... I'm..."

"I've got you," he says, gripping me tight. Claiming me. Loving me. "Come for me."

Energy crackles beneath my skin, setting off a chain of explosions that have me clenching around his cock so hard he comes right along with me. I shake against him, the after-shocks making my body jerk against him as the waves ebb.

Then he's kissing me, claiming my mouth the way he just did my body. I lose myself in his kiss, in the fullness I feel from having all my mates at once. It's overwhelming in the *best* way, and my body is barely solid as he moves us away from the wall and back to the cushions lining the floor.

Hands and arms and legs tangle, until we're one big pile, catching our breath and radiating in the aftereffects of pleasure.

As I lay there in the embrace of my mates, I feel, for the first time in a long time, that we're finally going to get our happily ever after.

And I can't wait to see what it looks like.

24

CARI

"I honestly never thought I'd ever set foot here," Huxton says as we walk through the All Plane garden. His golden eyes are even brighter with the sun shining high above us.

"I'm so glad you two were able to come," I say, looping my arm through Wynter's as she walks next to me.

"It's pretty," she says. "But I'm not going to buy a house or anything." She wrinkles her nose at the sky. "The sun is not my favorite."

I laugh, nodding. "It took me a while to get used to as well."

She grins. "I'm sure it was a lot easier with four mates as motivation."

"That is true," I admit with another laugh. We stroll through the garden, both of them stopping every so often to admire the All Plane flowers.

"Is this where Gessi planted the All Cure?" Huxton asks when we reach the end of the garden, and the newest addition.

Right now, it's just a large rectangular patch of upturned

earth, but in a few months' time, it should be sprouting with All Cure flowers.

"Yes," I say. "She did it when she visited shortly after the war ended." My heart pangs with a longing that only missing one's best friend can do, but it's flooded by so much happiness it's hard to feel sad. It's been a month since she visited, and two since we defeated the general.

The Shattered Isle is restored, and the All Plane is continuing to grow in alliances, though we are still on fragile ground when it comes to the Stone Realm's loyalty, but we're working toward peace. Same with the Corters.

"Have you thought of a debt I can repay yet?" I ask Huxton as we head back to the palace.

He smiles at me, shaking his head. "Not as of yet, queen," he says, dipping his head a little.

"Please stop calling me that," I say, waving him off as we enter the palace. "If it weren't for you, both our realms would've suffered." We've already given the Onyx City a healthy donation of resources and goods in an attempt to repay him for his services during the war. I know I still owe him, but he has yet to demand a payment. "And I consider you and Wynter friends. After all you've done...please, it's just Cari."

"I have no problem calling you Cari," Wynter says as we stop in the dining hall. She bites into a strawberry, shrugging at Huxton's shocked look. "What?" she asks. "She's not my queen."

"Wynter," Huxton chides, but she just arches a brow at him.

I laugh, eying the two as they stare each other down. They look like they're having a silent argument, communicating like Lock and I do. I press my lips together, shaking my head.

"Huxton, it's fine," I say, and the tension eases from his shoulders just a bit. "She's right. I'm not her queen." And that is something I never thought I'd say—I'm not a Shattered Isle queen.

My best friend is.

I'm queen of the All Plane.

My once upon a time enemies.

"Are you sure I can't convince you two to stay any longer?" I ask after we've snacked in comfortable silence for a few moments.

"As much as I would love to," Huxton says. "The Onyx City needs me."

I nod, wrapping him in a warm hug. They've already been here a week—it's selfish of me to want to keep my new friends here any longer. His city is the second largest in the Shattered Isle, and after all the changes that he underwent in the war—housing victims of the war and supplying us with his armies—he has his work cut out for him getting things back to normal.

"Thank you again," I say, moving to hug Wynter. "For everything."

Huxton nods, and Wynter hugs me back. "There is a girls' trip for you, me, and Gessi in the future," she says, releasing me. "I mean it. Somewhere fun we've all never been. Deal?"

"Deal," I say, then eye Huxton. "And if you ever think of that debt—"

"You'll be the first to know," he cuts me off.

"I'll hold you to that," I say, and they both head off to their rooms to finish packing their things, their ship already prepped to leave before we ventured out to the garden.

A settled happiness steals over me, filling my lungs with a much-needed deep breath. Things are falling into place, finally, after all the death and destruction we've lived through. Nightmares still jerk me from sleep with memories of the general, memories of almost losing Lock, losing Steel, but I'm working through the trauma one day at a time.

Lock is helping me, using his gifts to help me go through old memories and get closure and clarity on them. I didn't realize how many I had of the general, of my father, and the tortures they inflicted, but we're getting through it as best we can.

Weaving through the palace, I dare a pass by Talon's work rooms, peeking through the partially cracked door. He's deep in work mode, and Storm is on a screen on the wall, giving reports and updates on the Stone Realm progress while Talon rushes from one table to the next.

I think about stepping in and saying hi to my friend, but the two look like they have their hands full, and I know better than to distract Talon's brilliant mind when he's in the zone.

I quietly shut the door and head down the hallway, my instincts guiding me as I make the twists and turns until I find him. I lean against the open door to his study, admiring him as he sits behind his desk, brow furrowed in concentration as he reads something on a tablet.

Stars, he's so damn beautiful sitting there, that muscle in his jaw flexing as he continues to read. Emotion spirals inside me, drawing up images from the battlefield, playing the horrific scene where the sword sunk into his chest behind my eyes. My heart clenches every single time. It doesn't matter that it's been two months. Doesn't matter that I've held him in my arms and kissed his lips a thousand times to assure myself that he's alive, he's healthy, he's here —it still hurts.

"Watching me work has to be the least entertaining

activity ever," Steel says without looking up from the tablet. "But here you are again."

I bite my lip when he finally looks up at me, his smile broad and breath-stealing.

"Can you truly blame me?" I ask, remaining in the doorway. "You make everything look so damn good."

Steel laughs, leaning back in his chair as he waves me inside. "Get in here, wife," he demands. I hurry inside, and he cocks a brow. "Lock the door."

A thrill shoots through me, and I flip the lock before rushing over to his desk.

Steel pushes back enough in his chair so I can easily slide into his lap. Our lips instantly meet, the kiss insatiable as we crash together. Feeling his mouth against mine, his powerful hands on my body, does everything to chase all those bad memories away.

"Am I taking you away from something important?" I ask between kisses. "I can come back later. I don't want to—"

"You're the most important thing in my world," Steel cuts me off.

He grips my hips, hefting me out of his lap and perching my ass on the edge of his desk as he stands up. Parting my thighs, he hikes my dress up and up until it bunches around my waist, his fingers warm against my skin.

I tangle my fingers in his hair, slamming my mouth against his again, shivering as he rubs my thighs in teasing strokes. I wiggle atop his desk, inching closer to his fingers, desperate for him to touch me where I need him most.

He draws his lips from mine. "You look like you need something, wife," he says, his voice low and rough. He drags a finger over the silk covering my pussy.

I jerk into the slight touch, my body spiraling with heat.

"You," I say, inching for his mouth again.

He pulls just out of reach, his blue eyes like molten sapphires. "Tell me how bad you need me."

"Bad," I sigh, arching my head back as he slips his fingers beneath my silk and curling them against my slit. "Really bad, Steel."

I lean back a little, supporting myself with my palms against his desk, trying to give him more access.

"Really bad, huh?" he breathes the words against my mouth, grazing his lips over mine as he slides a finger inside me, then another, working them in and out of me until I shiver.

"Yes," I groan, one hand flying to his muscled bicep, gripping it as he pumps his fingers into me. "Stars, *yes*."

"You're so wet for me, wife," he says, slanting his mouth over mine. His tongue strokes into my mouth in time with his fingers, and my entire body responds to the touch. Nerves spark to life, twisting and tightening with each graze of his touch.

"Steel," I say against his mouth, breathless as he works me up. I rock into his hand, riding it as I try and relieve the pressure building up inside me.

His lips are warm against mine, kissing me, loving me, stroking me to absolute perfection. Everything builds and builds inside me, all at the mercy of Steel's touch until I can hardly breathe around the pressure.

"I know what you need," he says, grinding the heel of his palm against my throbbing clit—

"Steel!" I cry out his name as I clench around his fingers, my entire body trembling as my orgasm shakes free. He swallows my cries with his mouth, his tongue sweeping inside and rubbing against mine as I shiver against him.

Gently, he pulls his fingers back, wetting his lips as he

grazes his eyes over me. My hands fly to his pants, working them down just enough to free his cock. It's hard and beautiful and I wrap my legs around his hips, jerking him forward in a move so fast and powerful he laughs as he crashes against me.

I smile up at him, never losing his gaze as I reach between us and maneuver his thick length right where I need him. I shiver again as I tease him, gliding the head of his cock through my slick heat, and I relish his groan as he presses his forehead against mine.

"Cari," he says my name like a plea, and I guide him inside me until he bottoms out.

"Stars, yes." He fills me, all hard heat and pulsing pleasure. "Fuck me, Steel."

His hands trail down my arms as he lifts them from the desk, wrapping them around his neck. "Hold on to me," he says, and lightning streaks through my veins at the command.

And then he unleashes himself on me. No holding back his power, his incredible strength, as he pulls all the way out of me and slams back in with two easy moves.

I gasp, clinging to him as he does it again.

And again.

Each thrust sends tendrils of heat along my body until another white-hot knot forms in my core. He grabs one of my hips, bracing his other hand on the desk as he pumps into me with hard, long strokes that have me *keening*.

The desk groans as he pounds into me, each time our bodies connect, my throbbing clit shudders with delight, sparking with energy as pleasure builds and twists in my body.

"*Cari*," he groans. "Sun above, mate. You feel so fucking good around my cock."

"Oh, stars," I moan, feeling release dance on the edge of my insides. "Steel, yes. Just like that."

He slows his pace, dragging his thick length through my heat, ensuring when he jerks back inside me, he hits my clit. I shake harder with each teasing, long stroke. He's winding me so tight, dragging out my pleasure until it almost hurts.

I love it.

"I love you," I breathe the words, gripping his neck and drawing his lips to mine as I rock against him. "I love you so much."

"I love you," he says against my lips, pumping into me with more intensity. "So fucking much." He accentuates the words with thrusts of his hips, and by the last one, I come completely undone for him.

My pussy flutters around his cock as he continues to pump inside me as I come, my body a mess of tingles and little explosions that have my breath coming in heaves as he ups his pace, pushing one orgasm into another until he spills inside me.

Our bodies are slick with sweat as we come down, Steel holding me against him as he gently moves us backward, him falling into his chair and me in his lap.

I cup his face, smiling at him before I kiss him again.

Simply because I *can*.

25

CARI

It's another hour before I leave Steel to his work.

And another four before I make my way to Lock's chambers—where I've been sleeping most nights.

The others understand the need for us to be together as much as possible. After all that's happened, it's been hard to let him or Steel out of my sight.

I make sure I'm spending equal time with Talon and Tor, ensuring my mates get all the attention and love they deserve, but they are fully supportive of my need to spend my nights with Lock solo.

"Darling," Lock says by way of greeting when I slip into his rooms. His bare feet are propped on an ottoman, a book between his hands as he lounges in his plush armchair in the corner near the balcony.

"Mate," I say, strolling straight for him. "Good chapter?" I ask when I reach his side, leaning over the armrest of the chair to kiss his cheek.

"Truly delightful," he says, slowly closing the book. "The villain of the story is falling in love with his enemy."

I smile at him, pulling away. "That sounds riveting," I

say, and he furrows his brow as I back up a few paces. "I don't want to pull you away from it." I turn on my heels and stride out onto the balcony, leaning against the railing.

The stars stretch out in a perfect midnight sky above me, the sky clear and glittering. Something soft as silk caresses my bare leg beneath my dress, and I gasp at the touch.

A low, warning growl rumbles in my ear before Lock materializes behind me from his shadows, his chest pressing against my back as his fingers grip my arms.

"How dare you turn your back on a monster," he says in my ear. I swear the words stroke the spot between my thighs. "Don't you know how dangerous that is?"

I tremble against him, tilting my head to the side as he kisses down my neck. "How dare *you* sneak up on a monster," I say, spinning in his embrace to face him. Frost kisses my fingers as I slip them beneath his shirt. He hisses in response to the cold, grinning down at me. "Don't you know how dangerous *that* is?"

His laugh is low and slow as he wraps his arms around my waist, hauling me to his eye level. "My brutal, beautiful mate," he says before gently kissing me. "I've missed you."

I shudder against him, kissing him back. He saw me this morning at our standing morning meeting, but I know what he means. We've yet to recover from our time apart. I'm not sure if I ever will. But he's here, now, in my arms. That's all that matters.

"Take me to bed?" I ask, and his smile is pure mischief as he shifts me until he's cradling me against his chest, carrying us to his bed.

"Sleep is the last thing on my mind, darling."

"Good," I say as he lays me down, his mouth meeting mine in an effortless move. I spear my fingers in his black hair, tangling them in the silky strands as we roll to our sides without breaking the kiss.

He hooks my leg around his hip, his hands roaming beneath my dress as he smooths them over my thigh. It's seconds before he removes the dress, and I rid him of his clothes too. I move atop him them, working my way down his body until I wrap my lips around his cock.

"*Darling*," he sighs the endearment, and I take him deeper into my mouth.

I suck and tease and drag the edges of my teeth along his shaft, relishing every flex of his fingers in my hair, loving every pleasured groan from his lips.

"Ah, ah," he chides me as his entire body tenses the faster I work at him. "The only place I'm coming tonight is inside you." His shadows encircle me, gently lifting my body from my position and spinning me until I'm on my back, Lock fully atop me.

"Cheater," I teased.

"I've never pretended to play fair." He lines up his cock with the center of me, bracing his muscled arms on either side of my head before inching inside me.

He pauses for a moment, letting me adjust to the size of him before he starts to move. Slow at first, then, as the heat in his gaze grows headier, he ups his pace, pumping into me with all the speed our desire demands.

His hands slip down and beneath me, gently clutch my ass, helping leverage me right where he wants me as I ride him from underneath. Stars, he's perfection—all dangerous looks and caressing shadows. And love. So much love radiates down the bond between us, blazing like the brightest star in a midnight sky.

I can't touch him enough, can't hold him enough, kiss him enough.

My body coils, pleasure swarming in knots all along my soul when I feel his gentle request at the edge of my mind. I open for him immediately, love pouring inside me that he still asks for permission even though I keep a space open for him indefinitely.

Lock's essence fills my mind, the snow and stars scent potent as I breathe him in. We stay right where we are, but we're connected in every way imaginable—mind, body, and soul.

His pleasure wraps around mine, magnifying it until everything in my world narrows to every spot we connect.

We're endless and always and I can't contain my cry as I flutter around him. My orgasm stretches wide along my body, making me tremble as he works me through the throes of it, as he drinks my moans and finds his own release inside me.

I wrap my arms around him as he turns us on our side, resting my head against his shoulder as we hold each other, catching our breath.

"Did that feel real to you?" I whisper the question as I look at him.

"Real enough for me," he says, grinning down at me before he seals our promises to each other with a kiss.

EPILOGUE
LOCK

Six Years Later

A burst of panic slices through me as I hurry down the hallway, my heart racing against my chest.

Not again. Cari is going to kill me—

"Boom!" Ella's little shriek makes me jump as she appears out of the shadows in the corner. My hand splays on my chest as I look down at her, laughing. "Got you, Daddy!"

I kneel to her level, tucking some of her long black hair behind her ears. Her little cheeks are the same blue as her mothers, but she has my green eyes. Shadows flicker behind her, weaving haphazardly back and forth since she doesn't quite have control of them yet.

"You certainly did," I say.

My daughter loves hide and seek, but damn, she's taken it to another level now that she's learned how to hide in her shadows. I almost lost her. Again. And that would not sit well with my mate. One time it took me an hour to find Ella, and Cari nearly turned me into an ice sculpture.

A zap of lightning cracks the air, the little shock landing

on Ella's arm. She squeaks, then growls as her brother races past her.

"You're it!" Oliver shouts over his shoulder.

Ella glares at her older brother. "No powers!" she hollers as she chases after him.

"Did she win again?" Cari asks from behind me, and I turn to smile at my wife. Fucking hell, she's gorgeous, her belly newly swollen as she runs a hand lovingly over it.

"Of course not," I say, wrapping my arm around her as we make our way down the hallway. "You know no one can outsmart me."

Cari laughs, the sound so full and rich. "Of course," she says, rolling her eyes as we turn into the dining hall.

Talon is smiling at Ella, pointing behind Tor where Oliver is trying and failing to hide.

Ella smiles from ear to ear, racing in that direction—

Steel scoops her up, holding onto her wiggling, giggling body while he shouts at Oliver to make a break for it.

Oliver shoots across the space, his lightning sparking from his little fingers before Tor darts into his path, spinning him around. "Face your fears, son," he says teasingly. "Don't run from them."

"I'm not afraid," Oliver says.

Steel releases Ella, and Oliver squeals and runs the opposite direction.

We all laugh at that, the five of us content to watch them play.

My chest expands with the scene. Sometimes I can't believe I'm here, experiencing things I never thought I would. Not only do I have the love and support of my brothers, but we have a family. From the way our fathers treated us, Cari and I weren't sure if we ever wanted children, but then Oliver came along, and then Ella, and we knew we'd be the loving parents we never had.

"She's getting better with them," Talon says to me, nodding toward where Ella is wielding her little shadows to sneak up on Oliver.

"She is," I say, swallowing hard. She's got the support I never had, and I'll work every day to ensure they all continue to have the best life I can offer them.

Steel comes to check on Cari, doting on her every whim as usual while Tor joins the battle raging across the room. Ella has him disarmed within seconds, which makes me smile.

I shift closer to Cari, smoothing my hand down her back, wondering how the hell I got so lucky, when something hits me dead center of my soul.

I freeze, the sensations flooding me with an unfamiliar tap against my mental shields. Carefully, I lower them, adjusting my powers to adapt to the new presence...

The *two* new presences.

The mental awareness isn't wholly there, but there is a feeling...love, curiosity, warmth.

I gasp, a joyful laugh tearing from my lips that is so out of place in the room that all heads turn to me except for Ella and Oliver, who keep playing. Tor hurries over, his brow furrowed.

"What is it?" Cari asks, and I can't help but fall to my knees before her, running my hands over her stomach. "Lock?" she asks, concern fluttering over her features.

Talon and Steel are looking down at me too, concern filling their eyes.

"I can feel them," I explain, my heart in my throat.

"*Them*?" Cari asks.

I close my eyes, focusing harder. I gently push my powers toward Cari, toward the lives inside her—

"Wow," I gasp, shaking my head as I smile, looking up at Steel. "They're strong," I continue. "So incredibly strong."

Tears glitter over his blue eyes, his lips parted, but no words come out.

"What else?" Cari asks, happy tears rolling down her cheeks.

"Love." I kiss her stomach. "They have so much love for you."

Cari's smile is bright as she reaches for Steel. He gently scoops her up, kissing her fiercely before setting her back on her feet. It's a beautiful moment, one I'm so grateful to be a part of. But then Cari spins around, her eyes on Talon. She crosses the distance between them.

"Are you okay?" she asks, and she doesn't need to explain further. Tor has a son, I have a daughter, and now Steel is having twins.

"Am I okay?" Talon asks, his usual stern demeanor disappearing as a grin stretches his lips. "We're having twins!" he says, pulling her against him. "I'm more than okay."

She breathes against him, kissing him.

"Besides," he says, kissing her back. "I'm more than happy to keep trying for our own."

A visible shudder wracks Cari's body, and I laugh. Not one of us would say no to our mate, ever.

Ella races up to me, leaping into my arms without so much as a warning. I catch her, hiking her up in my arms so her face is level with mine.

Oliver bounds over to Talon, dragging him away from Cari. "Can I play in your workshop, Dad?" he asks, and Talon of course gives in as the two head out of the room.

Tor laughs, following them.

"Daddy," Ella says as I head toward the doors, wanting to give Steel and Cari a private moment to enjoy the news. "Can you tell me about the time you met Mommy?"

"Again?" I ask, glancing over my shoulder at Cari. She smiles at me where we stand in the doorway, and I wink at her before heading out of the room and down the hallway.

"Yes, please," she says, leaning her head against my shoulder, the chase with her brother clearly having worn her out.

I make the way toward her bedchambers, settling her back on her mattress and tucking her in for a nap. "Well, a long time ago, way before you were born, your mother set me free..."

I leave out the more gruesome details of our story, focusing only on the good parts. I've told Ella this version of the story so much, I'm beginning to believe it's actually the way we met. No battles, no scars, no wars, just us.

Ella's eyes are almost closed by the time I finish, my voice practically a whisper. I quietly stand up beside her bed, looking down at my daughter—she's a perfect combination of Cari and myself, and I never knew I could love anything as much as I love her.

"Darling," I whisper.

"Yes, Daddy?" she asks, her eyes shutting.

"How much does Daddy love you?"

"More than there are stars in the sky," she answers sleepily, and I lean down to kiss her forehead.

"That's right," I say, pausing in her doorway, watching as she falls fully asleep.

My stars in an endless night sky.

I turn out of her room, gently shutting the door, and head down the hallway in search of my mate. I need to thank her for all she's given me, for saving me, and most importantly, for setting me free.

THE END

THANK you so much for reading! If you haven't read the first two books in the series featuring Cari and her mates be sure to check out HER VILLAINS and HER REVENGE in Kindle Unlimited!

Read the third book in the Shattered Isle series, THE ASSASSINS, here. It focuses on Gessi and her assassins!

If you're looking for 75 pages of pure smutt with Cari and her mates, check out the spicy novella HER MATES here.

LET'S CHAT!

I love hearing from you! You can find me at the following places!

TikTok @JadePresleyAuthor
Instagram
Facebook
Facebook Author Page
Jadempresley@gmail.com
LinkTree
BookBub
And be sure to sign up for my newsletter here for release information, cover reveals, and giveaways!

ACKNOWLEDGMENTS

Have to give a huge shout out to my newest Patron subscribers: Morgan, Daleina, Alisha , Jacqulin, Sarah, Lucinda, Brittani Bone, Mai, Jael, & Lindsay!!

A GIANT thank you must be paid to all the amazing, badass booktokers out there that have been so amazing and supportive! The list below is just a snapshot of the wonderful readers out there and if I missed your name, PLEASE know that I see you and appreciate every mention, video, comment, and message! I love you all!

@chelsluca @sarahsbooksandhobbies @here4allthebooks @brittalways_reads @o3mustangmomma @kalpal97 @duudeidk @mia__boudreau @emilywhite552 @tin-kerthewriter @julieelliee @darkrosereads_93 @natashareadsshit @romance_book_aesthetics @ashlee-boldingreads @buckyspersonalmilf @ryann.thebusyreader @literarylifebyhaylee @tiffandbooks @daniisbookish @win-terarrow @trishaarwood @pixiepages @oliveroseandco @thebookishgirlreviews @asthebookends @breanna_reads @booksdanirreads @songreads @erynsarchive @yelena-books @hdouglas92 @leggothemeggoreads @klaudias_-bookdiary @libraryofmadison @stakestheworld @thebookcloud @spicybooks @sami_cantstopreading @rachies_book_nook @dealingdreams @bookloving-corgimom @coffeeandbookswithlauran @lokiquinn1993 @nightowlbooks @bookofcons @animebaby33 @muddy_orbs @crysreads @biblio_mama @briannareadds @morallygrayreads @fortheloveofbooksandwine @natashareadsnrambles @pagel_bagel_ @nerdy_julith @bookishmot @jvstjewels @breereadsromance_ @moon-noodledesigns @thebookishlifeofchels @touch.my.shelf @once.upon.a.bookshelf @dani.reads.books @dumbSong @ireadromancetoescape @spidersamii @jazzyjay121 @six-horizonreads @da_vincis_daughter @mary_a_light_official @beautyandthebookcase @rachelptrsm12 @the_bookish-siren @nicolasbooks @thatreadingmom @feral.for.fiction @katiemurphy18 @readswithcoffee @the8thhorcurx @chelsbellsbooklover @candicereads @mjmona89 @raquel.reads @meggintheempath @bookishvader @thiscrazy-bookishlife @hreads2much @ashtonthescorpio @e_paletta @nofergirl @jaclynoiler @laney1811 @booktok.books1011 @helenwyn43 @sassyboots4

Another huge thanks to Amber Hodge for editing this and making it sparkle! I couldn't do this series without you!

A big thanks to my husband and family who always indulge me when I get lost in the writing cave.

And finally, a huge shout out to all the Marvel fans who just want a little more sometimes :)

Made in the USA
Middletown, DE
01 June 2023

31904152R00136